Read-Aloud
Children's Classics

publications international, ltd.

Contents

✎ Puss in Boots ✎

Adapted by Jamie Elder ▪ Illustrated by Susan Spellman

Puss was a clever cat who belonged to an old farmer. But one day, the old farmer died. Puss was very sad. He did not want to be all alone. He needed someone to take care of him. He needed to take care of someone.

Puss chose the farmer's youngest son.

Puss approached the young man. The young man had a very worried look on his face. He had many things on his mind. Puss remembered that the old farmer looked the same way once. The farmer was always worried before Puss had helped him. Puss knew just what to do.

"Please take me home with you," Puss said to the young man.

"I can't take you home with me," said the young man.

"Why not?" Puss asked.

"Because I have many things on my mind," said the young man.

"No need to worry," Puss said. "I am not much trouble."

"I can't help you," said the young man.

"But I can help you," Puss said.

"How can you help me?" the young man asked.

"Just give me a pair of boots. I can help," Puss said.

The young man laughed, but Puss just smiled.

"All right," said the young man. "Come home with me. It couldn't hurt to have a cat that makes me laugh."

Puss happily followed the young man home. When they reached his farm, Puss stopped smiling. He could see why the young man was worried. It was not much of a farm. Puss would have to be more clever than he thought.

"Will the boots be very much trouble?" Puss asked.

"I have an extra pair," the young man said.

"Do you think maybe you have an old sack, too?" Puss asked.

"I am sure I do," the young man said. "But why?"

Puss did not want to explain. He did not want to ruin any surprises. Instead of answering, he just smiled again. The young man shrugged and laughed. He found his extra boots. He found an old sack.

"Thank you very much," Puss said.

"You are very welcome," said the young man.

Puss waved to the young man and walked towards the forest. On the way, he gathered some good grass. He put the grass in the sack. When he found a nice tree, he put the sack down. He tried on his boots, and they were very comfortable. Then he pretended to be asleep.

Soon a rabbit came by. He nosed the sack open and found the good grass. When he crawled inside to eat it, Puss jumped up. He tied the sack so the rabbit could not escape.

Smiling again, he began to walk to the kingdom's castle. It felt good to be so clever. He just hoped things would work out.

∾ Puss in Boots ∾

At the castle, Puss asked to see the king. He was led to the throne room. Many people were in attendance around the king. Puss almost forgot his plan.

"State your business," said the king.

"Your Majesty," Puss began, "I have brought you a gift from my master."

"Who is your master?" asked the king.

"Your Majesty, my master is the duke of Cataclaws," Puss said.

The king was a good king, but he was very forgetful. His forgetfulness was known throughout the kingdom. Puss was very clever, and his cleverness was a secret. His master was only the young man. The young man was not a duke. Puss just wanted the king to think he was a duke. Puss hoped everyone in attendance was forgetful, too.

"What is the gift?" asked the king.

"Your Majesty, it is a fine, fat rabbit. The duke of Cataclaws wanted you to have a fine feast," Puss said.

"Thank your master for me," said the king. "I accept his gift with pleasure."

Puss bowed to the king and smiled. Everything was working out just fine. Puss returned to the castle the next day. He brought two plump birds from the duke of Cataclaws. The king was pleased.

The king was pleased with everything Puss brought him that week. Each time, he told Puss to thank the duke of Cataclaws. At the end of the week, Puss was satisfied. He knew the king would not forget the duke of Cataclaws.

11

Puss returned home with a plan. It was hard to wait for the right moment. Until he could do more, he tried to amuse the young man.

"Can you stand on your head?" Puss asked him.

"No," said the young man. "Can you?"

"Can I stand on your head?" Puss asked. "Sure!"

Puss perched on top of the young man's head. They laughed. Then the right moment came. The king's carriage was coming down the road!

"Go down to the river," Puss said to the young man. "When you get there, take off all your clothes and jump in."

"What are you up to? First, boots and a sack. Now this," he said.

Puss pushed the young man towards the river. Then he ran after the king's carriage.

"Help! Help! The duke of Cataclaws has been thrown into the river!"

The king poked his head out of the carriage. "The duke of Cataclaws?" he asked.

"Yes, Your Majesty! The duke was robbed and is drowning," Puss said.

"We must help him," said the king. "He has been so good to me."

The carriage raced to the river. The water was swift. The king ordered his guards to rescue the duke of Cataclaws.

During the rescue, Puss saw the king's daughter inside the carriage. He knew then that things were working out well.

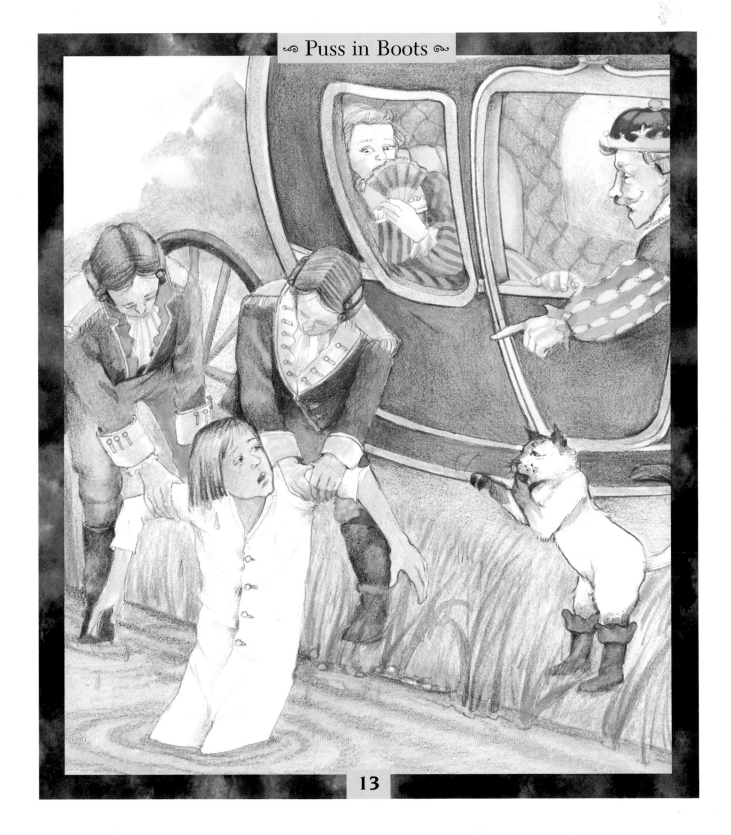

Puss went to the carriage and peeked inside. The beautiful princess was sitting inside the carriage. She was very concerned for the young man.

"Is he all right?" she asked Puss.

"I think he will be fine," Puss said. "Of course, his clothes have been stolen. I hope he will not catch a cold."

"Nonsense," said the king. "I will have clothes brought to him."

The king sent a guard back to the castle. The guard returned with a suit of clothes. The young man put it on and looked rather fine. In fact, he looked just like a real duke.

Puss was so pleased that his plan was working.

"You must come with us," said the king.

"We are taking a tour of the kingdom," said the princess.

The young man looked at Puss. He was very confused. Puss had to think quickly to explain the young man's silence.

"The duke is humbled by your invitation," Puss said.

"Please enjoy this time with us," said the princess.

"He is delighted to be among you," Puss said.

"Thank you," the young man finally said.

Puss jumped down from the side of the carriage. The young man stepped inside. Puss ran ahead of the carriage.

His work was really just beginning.

Puss ran fast to carry out his plan. He had to speak to everyone along the way. He came upon two farmhands first.

"You are working very hard," Puss said to the farmhands.

"These are the giant's fields. We must work hard or be cut into pieces," the first man said.

"Actually, that is why I am here," Puss said.

"You are going to cut us into pieces?" the second man asked.

"No!" Puss said. "I am only here to tell you about the giant. The king has just made him the duke of Cataclaws."

"There is the king's carriage now," said the first man.

"Yes," said Puss. "The king will ask you who owns this land. If you say the duke of Cataclaws, the king will be impressed. He will know the giant cares about his title. In turn, the giant will be pleased with you for being so clever. You may not have to work so hard."

"It would be nice not to have to work so hard," the second man said.

"What would happen if you told the king the wrong thing?" Puss asked.

"We would be cut into pieces," the first man said.

"Here comes the king now," Puss said.

The farmhands bowed to the king as he approached.

"Who owns this land?" asked the king as the carriage stopped.

"The duke of Cataclaws," both men said at the same time.

Puss could see that the king was pleased. The king believed the young man was the duke. Puss could see the young man and the princess. They were smiling at each other.

Puss waved to everyone and ran ahead. His biggest task was before him. He had to take care of the giant. He hoped again to be clever enough. He did not want to be cut into pieces. He just wanted to help the young man.

He arrived at the giant's castle and demanded to see him. Inside a huge hall, the giant sat on a stool. He did not look very comfortable. Puss did not feel bad about that.

"I hear you have special powers," Puss said.

The giant sneered at him.

"That's what I thought," Puss said. "I didn't believe what I heard."

"What did you hear?" the giant asked.

"I heard you could turn into any sort of animal," Puss said.

"It is true," the giant said.

"But probably not a great lion, right?" Puss asked.

The giant answered him by turning into a great lion. Puss was a little bit frightened. For the giant, he pretended to be really scared.

"A lion is a great thing to turn into. You probably don't bother with small animals, though," Puss said.

"Not usually," the giant said.

"That's right," Puss said. "I didn't think so. I knew you couldn't turn into something like a mouse. That would be impossible."

The giant growled at Puss. Puss thought he was about to be cut into pieces. Instead, the giant turned into a tiny mouse.

Puss wasted no time. He pounced on the mouse. He opened his mouth and gobbled it up.

There was no more giant.

He was able to do it just in time, too. The king's carriage arrived at the castle just at that moment. Puss ran to greet it.

"Welcome to the castle of the duke of Cataclaws!" Puss said.

"This is your fine castle?" the king asked the young man.

The young man looked at Puss. Puss smiled at him and nodded. He hoped the young man trusted him enough. He had been very clever. All he wanted was to help the young man.

The young man turned to the king. He smiled and nodded just like Puss had done.

"Won't you come inside?" the young man asked.

It was then that Puss knew everything was going to be fine. He had been clever enough. He had helped the young man. The young man was never meant to be a farmer. He was meant to be a duke.

And Puss knew he would like being a duke's cat.

❧ The Nightingale ❧

Adapted by Brian Conway ▪ Illustrated by Robin Moro

he emperor of China had the most beautiful palace. People came from all over the world to see it.

The rooms were huge. The windows were covered with draperies of the finest silk. The rugs were made by the best craftsmen in the world. The furniture was of the highest quality.

One hundred gardeners worked in the palace gardens. They took care of thousands of plants. They grew and tended the rarest flowers.

People came to see these beautiful things. They wanted to see things they had never seen before. They toured the palace and the gardens and were amazed at every turn. They wanted to see more when the tour was over.

"Don't let our trip end," they said.

The head gardener heard them. He knew where there was something more beautiful than any palace. It was more beautiful than any garden.

"I can show you the most beautiful thing in all of China," he said.

He led the visitors to a forest of very plain trees. He took them to one tree in particular. He pointed at a bird on a branch. The visitors looked up.

"What is so beautiful about that?" they asked. "You led us all the way out here? You wanted us to see a plain gray bird?"

"It is no ordinary bird," the gardener said. "It is a nightingale. Just wait."

The nightingale opened his mouth. He started to sing. His voice was beautiful. The nightingale made everyone feel joy.

The visitors left with the memory of the nightingale's song.

The nightingale became known as the most beautiful thing in all of China. Everyone had heard about the remarkable bird.

Everyone, that is, except for the emperor.

The emperor was very old. He stayed inside. He liked his palace. He liked the view of his gardens. But nothing brought him joy.

One day, the emperor received a letter from the emperor of Japan.

"I have heard of your wonderful nightingale," the emperor of Japan wrote. "Some people say he is the most beautiful thing in all the world. I must see this wonderful bird. I will arrive in two days to pay you a visit."

The emperor was puzzled. He called for his prime minister.

"The emperor of Japan is coming to see my nightingale," he said. "He thinks I have a nightingale. I do not have a nightingale. What will I show the emperor of Japan when he arrives?"

The emperor called all of his guards together.

"Find me this beautiful nightingale," he said.

His guards tried to do as they were told. They searched through every inch of the palace. They could not find the bird.

No one knew where to look next.

No one, that is, except the head gardener. He knew where to find the nightingale. He took everyone to the nightingale's tree.

The guards hurried back from the woods. They took the bird to the emperor's throne room.

"Well," said the emperor, "what is so special about this nightingale?"

"We do not know," they answered. "It is an ordinary bird. We found the bird in an ordinary tree."

A horn sounded just then. The emperor of Japan had arrived.

"Do not let the bird out of your sight," said the emperor.

He went to greet his visitor.

"I have come a long way," said the emperor of Japan. "I cannot wait to see the wonderful nightingale!"

The emperor took his guest to the throne room.

"This is the famous nightingale?" asked the emperor of Japan. "This is the most beautiful thing in all of China? The bird looks rather plain to me."

The emperor of Japan looked disappointed. The emperor of China was not enjoying his visitor.

There was silence in the throne room.

The nightingale opened his mouth. He sang the most beautiful song anyone had ever heard.

The emperor of Japan closed his eyes to listen. He smiled and sighed.

The emperor of China closed his eyes to listen, too. He felt something he had not felt in a long time. He felt joy.

The emperor of Japan stayed for several more days. He listened to the nightingale for hours. The emperor of China listened with him. They never grew tired of the nightingale's song.

After several days, the emperor of Japan had to leave China.

"Thank you for letting me hear this magnificent bird," he said. "I must find a way to thank you."

The nightingale's song filled the entire palace. It always brought the old emperor great joy.

It also brought visitors from all over the world.

No one wanted to see the emperor's palace or his gardens. They cared only for the nightingale.

"The nightingale sounds so lovely," the visitors said. "It is a pity he looks so plain."

Those words upset the emperor. The nightingale's song brought him joy. He was happier than he had ever been before.

"I will not allow any unkind words about the nightingale," he said.

The emperor ordered a golden perch for the nightingale to sit on. He ordered jewels and ribbons for the nightingale to wear.

"Now he will have a fine place to sit. He will look wonderful. But it is his beautiful song that counts," he said.

"The bird looks almost as beautiful as he sounds," the visitors said.

The nightingale sat on his golden perch. He wore his jewels. He wore his ribbons. He sang his song. He gave many people great joy. He was nice to watch and to listen to.

But the emperor thought the nightingale looked unhappy.

"Are you tired from singing?" the emperor asked.

The nightingale continued to sing.

"You must not sing if you are tired," the emperor said to the bird. "I want you to be happy."

The nightingale continued to sing.

"You are a dear friend," the emperor said.

The emperor kept the nightingale in his private chambers at night. There were no golden perches to sit on. There were no jewels and ribbons to be worn. The nightingale could just be himself.

The nightingale perched on the emperor's bedpost. He sang his songs only for the emperor.

"You are the most beautiful thing in all of China," the emperor said. "Gold and jewels and ribbons make you look nice. They do not make you beautiful. You are most beautiful when you are yourself. You are yourself when you are singing."

The nightingale sang a special song for the emperor. The emperor felt pure joy. He drifted off to sleep.

A package arrived for the emperor. It was a present. It was from the emperor of Japan. There was a card on the package.

"I hope you enjoy this gift," it read. "It is a small token of my gratitude. You gave me a wonderful gift. The nightingale gave me great joy."

The emperor of China opened the present.

It was a small toy bird. It was brightly painted. The bird was covered with emeralds, sapphires, diamonds, and rubies. There was a silver key on the bird's back.

The emperor tuned the key. A song began to play. It did not sound as lovely as the real nightingale. But it would make the visitors very happy. It was very beautiful to look at.

The emperor ordered a second golden perch. He placed the toy bird upon it. He turned the key.

"Now you will have some rest," the emperor said to the nightingale.

The visitors were thrilled.

"Finally!" they said. "A nightingale that looks as lovely as it sounds!"

The toy did not sound as beautiful as the nightingale. No one seemed to care. They asked for the toy to be wound over and over again.

The nightingale no longer sang. He flew home to the forest.

No one even noticed that the nightingale was gone.

No one, that is, except for the emperor. He missed his dear friend.

The emperor longed to hear the nightingale's beautiful song.

"I know my little friend likes the forest," he said. "It is for the best. I just hope he is happy."

The emperor's visitors were happy. They loved the toy bird's song. They especially loved the way it looked.

"Wind it again!" they said.

The emperor's servants wound the toy bird over and over again. It played all day. It played every day. It even played at night.

But something popped inside the bird one morning. There was a loud 'twang. The toy bird stopped playing.

The emperor shook the bird. The prime minister wiggled the key on its back. Everyone waited, but the toy bird would not play.

It was broken.

The emperor's watchmaker was summoned to the palace. He took the toy bird apart. He found out what was wrong.

"A spring has sprung," said the watchmaker. "This toy is broken."

"Can you fix it?" asked the emperor.

"Of course," said the watchmaker.

"Will it take long?" the prime minister asked. "The visitors love it."

"Not long," said the watchmaker. "But special care must be taken. It should be wound only on special occasions."

The palace became an unhappy place after that. There was no joy. No one came to visit anymore.

The emperor was sad and lonely.

He missed his friend the nightingale. He missed his beautiful song. He missed his company.

The emperor grew sick and weak. He stayed in bed.

The guards could not cheer him up. The servants could not cheer him up. The gardeners could not even cheer him up with a rare flower. No one could help the emperor.

No one, that is, except the head gardener. He knew the nightingale could help. He went to visit the nightingale.

"Your friend is ill," he said. "You should go and see him."

The nightingale flew to the emperor's window. The emperor rubbed his eyes. He smiled for the first time in a long time.

"You came back!" he said.

The nightingale opened his mouth. He sang a new song for the emperor. Tears of joy streamed down the emperor's cheeks. It was the most beautiful song he had ever heard.

He sat up in bed. The color returned to his face. He was happy to see his friend again. He knew he would hear the nightingale's sweet and special songs many more times.

❧ The Boy Who Cried Wolf ❧

Adapted by Jennifer Boudart   Illustrated by Jon Goodell

*T*he village of Woolington was known for sheep. Everybody had at least one. The doctor, the butcher, the blacksmith, and the mayor all had sheep.

What was so great about Woolington sheep? Their wool, of course! The town held a wool sale every spring. Buyers came from near and far. They came from everywhere. They brought empty carts and full pockets. They left with full carts and empty pockets.

"Woolington wool is so soft!" said some.

"It makes such warm blankets and sweaters," said others.

There was no question about it. Woolington loved its sheep. No one in Woolington loved them more than Timothy. He was the shepherd boy.

"I love the sheep," Timothy always said.

Timothy took his job very seriously. Each day, he gathered all the town's sheep. He walked them down the street. He herded them to the meadow.

Timothy found the sheep the greenest grass and the coolest water. He pulled rocks from their hooves. He combed their wool.

Woolington was very proud of Timothy.

"Timothy is a terrific shepherd," said the doctor.

"Timothy treats those sheep like family," said the butcher.

"Timothy always keeps the sheep safe," said the blacksmith.

"Timothy will not let us down," said the mayor.

Timothy's father had taught him everything about herding sheep.

"A shepherd boy must keep his sheep safe," Timothy's father said. "That is the first rule."

Timothy never forgot that rule. While he was on the job, he did not take a nap. He did not read a book. He only watched for trouble.

Maybe he did daydream a little. But he never had any real trouble. A lamb might try to run away. A dog might scare the sheep. A sheep might get its foot stuck in a hole. Those were small things.

"Watch out for wolves," Timothy's father said.

But Timothy had never seen a wolf in the meadow. He had never seen a wolf anywhere.

"Wolves must live way up in the mountains," he thought.

Timothy could see Woolington from the meadow. He watched people open their shops. He watched them hang out their wash. He watched them eat lunch. He watched other children play.

Timothy was bored sometimes. Every day was exactly the same. Get the sheep. Walk with the sheep. Watch the sheep. Take the sheep home. Timothy wanted to play like the other children.

Timothy tried to play with the sheep. He found out they were not very playful. They just chewed the grass when he kicked a ball. They just twitched their tails when he told a joke. The sheep did not want to play.

Timothy was sitting in the meadow one morning. He looked up at the sky. He gave each cloud a name for its shape. Flower cloud. Butterfly cloud. Wagon wheel cloud. Wolf cloud.

The last cloud gave him an idea. What would he do if a wolf came along? He had only his shepherd's crook. He was not very big. The wolf would not be scared of him. Timothy would be scared of the wolf.

What would he do? He could call for help. The people of Woolington would hear him. He had a very loud voice. Everyone would run down the street. They would rush into the meadow. The wolf would run away.

There would be three cheers for the shepherd boy. For him!

Timothy stood up. What if he pretended to see a wolf? Would the people of Woolington come running? That would be fun and exciting. Fun and excitement were just what he needed.

"Help! Help!" Timothy yelled. "A wolf is after the sheep!"

It was not true. All the sheep were there. They were eating grass. They did not even notice when he ran behind a tree.

Timothy watched people run from their shops. They dropped their wash. They left their lunches behind. Even the children stopped playing.

"Timothy needs help!" the people said.

Everyone ran to the meadow. The Woolington sheep were in trouble. Their shepherd boy was in trouble!

Never had there been so many people in the meadow. They all rushed up the hill. Their shouts filled the air.

All the sheep were there. The people of Woolington were confused.

"What is this?" asked the doctor.

"I do not see a wolf!" said the butcher.

"The only thing out of place is Timothy," said the blacksmith.

"Maybe the wolf dragged him away!" said the mayor.

That got everyone shouting and running again. They looked for wolf tracks. They looked for any clues about what had happened. One boy spotted Timothy's crook. It was next to a big tree. He ran to pick it up.

"Timothy is here," he said

Everyone looked at the big tree. Timothy came out from behind it. He took a few steps and fell down. He was shaking all over.

"Are you all right, Timothy?" the boy asked.

"I can't stop laughing!" Timothy said. "All that running and shouting! You all looked like a bunch of sheep! You looked like you were scared silly!"

"We were scared silly," said the mayor. "Now we are angry. Making up stories about wolves is not funny. Do not play tricks like that again."

Timothy tried to say he was sorry. His giggles got in the way. He could not stop laughing.

Everyone went back to town.

When Timothy got home, there was big trouble. His father was angry.

"I didn't want to upset anyone," Timothy said. "But it was a good test. I wanted to know what would happen if there was a wolf."

Timothy also thought it had been very funny. But he did not say that.

Timothy collected the sheep the next day. People were still angry.

"I worry about these sheep every day," he said to himself. "It was nice to have people worrying about me for a change."

He was angry that nobody worried about him. He was so angry he made a decision. He led the sheep to the meadow. Then he started yelling.

"Help!" he yelled. "A real wolf has come! He is after the sheep!"

Timothy found another place to hide. The town came running. They knew right away they had been tricked.

"Come out, Timothy," said the mayor.

Timothy had never seen the mayor so angry. He went to stand in front of him. He was not laughing anymore.

"You let us down," said the mayor. "We told you not to play tricks. You did not listen. Maybe we won't believe you if you call for help again."

Timothy felt bad. The mayor was right. He had been doing more than playing tricks. He had been telling lies.

"No more lies," Timothy said.

Only the sheep heard him. Everyone else had gone back to town.

A few days passed. Timothy took extra good care of the sheep. He wanted to prove he was still a good shepherd. He sat and watched for trouble. He also daydreamed a little.

Timothy heard a strange noise during one of his daydreams. It came from one of the sheep. It was not a happy sound. It was a frightened sound.

A wolf was in the meadow! A huge wolf! It was chasing the Woolington sheep. The wolf was biting the sheep. Timothy could see its sharp teeth.

"Help! Help!" Timothy yelled. "A wolf is in the meadow! It's chasing all the sheep!"

Timothy watched for someone to come running. No one did. He called for help again.

"A real wolf has come!" he yelled. "I am not making it up! I need help!"

Timothy was shouting as loud as he could. Timothy was jumping up and down. He was waving his arms. No one even turned to look at him. The town of Woolington might as well have been miles away.

Timothy could hear the wolf growling. He shook his crook at the wolf.

"Go away!" he said.

The wolf was not afraid, but Timothy was.

"Someone please help me!" he yelled.

There was no answer. Timothy was very afraid.

He ran all the way to Woolington.

He ran from one person to the next person.

"A wolf is in the meadow!" he said.

"Stop your tricks, Timothy," they all said.

Timothy ran to the doctor.

"A wolf is in the meadow!" he shouted.

"I am not a fool," said the doctor.

Timothy ran to the butcher shop.

"A wolf is in the meadow!" he shouted.

"Very funny, Timothy. Go back to the sheep," said the butcher.

Timothy ran to the blacksmith shop.

"A wolf is in the meadow!" he shouted.

"I don't want to hear another word," said the blacksmith.

Timothy even tried to talk to the mayor. The mayor just walked away.

"I am telling the truth!" he yelled.

No one paid attention. No one believed him. He started to cry.

Timothy remembered what the mayor had said.

"Maybe we won't believe you if you call for help again," he had said.

If only Timothy had not played tricks!

He ran back to the meadow. The wolf was gone. The Woolington sheep were gone, too. The wolf had taken them all away. Timothy had broken the first rule. He had not kept the sheep safe.

Nothing was the same after the day the wolf came. It became known as Wolf Day.

After Wolf Day, Woolington was no longer famous for sheep. No one kept sheep after that.

After Wolf Day, Timothy was no longer known as the shepherd boy. He was known as the boy who cried wolf. He was also known as the street sweeper. That was the only job he could get.

Timothy was very sorry about what had happened. It did not change things. He could not bring the sheep back.

Timothy took many walks to the meadow. He sat against a tree. He did not take a nap. He did not read a book. He did not even daydream. He thought about what had happened.

He took out his pocket knife. He used it to cut into the tree trunk. He carved a message there. You can still see it today if you visit Woolington.

This is what it says:

The boy who cried wolf lost the sheep of this town.

His tricks and his lies let Woolington down.

He joked about wolves, then a real one came by.

"It's a wolf," cried the boy. They said, "It's a lie."

The boy lost the sheep. He learned something, too.

If you want to be trusted, you must always be true.

The North Wind

Adapted by Lisa Harkrader ■ Illustrated by Beth Foster Wiggins

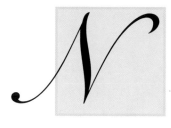ate's mother handed him a leather money pouch. The pouch had only a few coins in it.

"Go to the village," she said. "Buy some oats for our dinner tonight."

Nate ran to the village because he was very hungry. He bought a basket of oats.

On the way home, the North Wind began to blow. He blew into Nate's basket. He blew the oats across the field. He blew and he blew. He blew until the oats were gone.

Nate stared at the empty basket.

"I can't go home without oats for our dinner," he said.

He returned to the village and bought more oats.

On the way home, the North Wind began to blow. He blew into Nate's basket. He blew the oats across the field. He blew and he blew. He blew until the oats were gone.

Once more, Nate returned to the village. Once more, he bought a basket of oats.

Once more, the North Wind began to blow. He blew into Nate's basket. He blew the oats across the field. He blew and he blew. He blew until the oats were gone.

Nate stared at his empty basket. He stared into his empty money pouch.

Nate went to bed hungry that night. He knew his mother was hungry, too. He could not fall asleep.

He climbed from his bed. He put on his boots and mittens. He put on his heavy winter coat. He tiptoed past his mother's bed. He tiptoed out of the cottage.

"I must find the North Wind," he said. "Maybe he will give back our oats. I hope he will give them back."

Nate walked through the night. He walked through the dark and the cold. Snow swirled around him. Leaves crunched under his feet.

He was scared. He had never been so far from home before. He hoped he was going the right way. He hoped he was doing the right thing.

He kept walking. He walked through the darkest part of the forest. He walked until he came to a house made of stones. It had to belong to the North Wind.

Nate knocked at the door. It squeaked open.

A wrinkled face peeked out. It was the North Wind! Nate knew him at once. He looked old. He looked tired. But he did not look scary. Nate thought he would be scary, but he was not. He looked very kind.

The North Wind stared at Nate.

"What is it?" he asked.

His voice whistled through the forest.

"Three times I bought oats," said Nate. "Three times you blew them away. I came to get my oats back."

"I don't have your oats," said the North Wind. "It is my job to blow the wind. Once I blow oats away, they are gone. They are scattered across the fields. But you were brave to come here. I'll give you this, instead."

The North Wind handed Nate a tablecloth.

"Tell it, 'Cloth! Cloth! Serve food!' You will never be hungry again," the North Wind said.

Nate thanked the North Wind and set out for home. He stopped at an inn for dinner.

He sat down in the dining room of the inn. He spread the cloth on the dinner table.

"Cloth! Cloth! Serve food!" he said.

A roast beef sprang from the cloth. Up popped potatoes, carrots, bread, and cake. Nate ate and ate.

The innkeeper stood in the doorway. He watched and smiled. He gave Nate the very best room.

"Sleep well," he said.

The next morning, Nate ran all the way home. He ran into the cottage. He spread the cloth on the table.

"Mother, look!" he said. "Cloth! Cloth! Serve food!"

Nate watched. His mother watched. The cloth did not do anything.

Nate ran his hands over the tablecloth. He smoothed out the wrinkles.

"Cloth! Cloth! Serve food!" he said.

The cloth still did not do anything.

"I don't understand," Nate said. "It worked at the inn. The innkeeper saw it. He could tell you."

"I think you have been tricked," his mother said.

"I think you are right," he said.

Nate pulled on his boots and mittens. He put on his heavy winter coat. He set out to find the North Wind.

He walked through the day. He walked through the cold. Bushes rustled. Trees moaned.

He was scared. He knew wild animals lived in the woods. He knew they were big animals. He knew they were hungry animals. But he and his mother were hungry, too.

He kept walking. He walked through the darkest part of the forest. He walked until he came to the house made of stones.

Nate knocked at the door. It squeaked open.

The North Wind peeked out. He was surprised to see Nate.

"What is it now?" he asked.

His voice howled through the forest.

Nate handed the tablecloth to the North Wind.

"It doesn't work," he said. "You tricked me."

"Why would I trick you?" he asked. "I blow the wind. I do not have time for tricks."

"The cloth doesn't work," Nate said.

"This isn't the cloth I gave you," said the North Wind. "This one is torn and stained. But you were brave to come here. I'll give you this, instead."

The North Wind handed Nate a piggy bank.

"Say to it, 'Bank! Bank! Make money!' You will never be poor again," the North Wind said.

Nate thanked the North Wind and set out for home. He stopped at the same inn for the night.

Nate held the bank in front of him.

"Bank! Bank! Make money," he said.

Coins dropped from the bank.

Nate handed the coins to the innkeeper.

The innkeeper watched and smiled. He gave Nate the very best room.

"Sleep well," he said.

The next morning, Nate ran all the way home. He ran into the cottage. He held out the bank.

"Mother, look!" he said. "Bank! Bank! Make money."

Nate watched. His mother watched. The piggy bank did not do anything.

Nate rubbed his hands over the piggy bank.

"Bank! Bank! Make money!" he said again.

The bank still did not do anything.

"I don't understand," said Nate. "It worked in the inn. The innkeeper saw it. He could tell you."

"I think you have been tricked," his mother said.

"I think you are right," he said.

Again, Nate pulled on his boots and mittens. He put on his heavy winter coat. He set out to find the North Wind.

He walked through the day. He walked through the cold. Owls hooted. Wolves howled.

He was scared. He was afraid of what the North Wind would think. He knew the North Wind would be angry at him. But he was more afraid he and his mother would go hungry.

He kept walking. He walked through the darkest part of the forest. He walked until he came to the house made of stones.

He knocked at the door. The door squeaked open.

The North Wind peeked out. He was startled to see Nate.

"You again!" he said. "What is it this time?"

His voice thundered through the forest.

Nate handed the piggy bank to the North Wind.

"It doesn't work," he said. "You tricked me again."

"I didn't trick you," he said. "I blow the wind. I don't have time for tricks."

"The bank doesn't work," Nate said.

"This isn't the bank I gave you," the North Wind said. "This piggy bank is chipped and cracked. Someone is tricking you, but it is not me."

"The innkeeper!" Nate said. "He tricked me. He waited until I was asleep. Then he stole the bank. He must have taken the tablecloth, too. He was always watching me."

"You were brave to come here," the North Wind said. "I have something that you can use against tricksters."

He handed Nate a rope.

"Tell it, 'Rope! Rope! Tie him up!' You'll never be tricked again," he said.

"Thank you," Nate said. "You have been very kind to me."

He set off for the inn with the magic rope.

When the innkeeper saw Nate, he smiled.

"What have you brought tonight?" he asked.

"Only this magic rope," said Nate.

The innkeeper smiled again. He gave Nate the very best room.

"Sleep well," he said.

Nate set the rope on a chair. He crawled into bed. He waited.

Nate's door squeaked open in the middle of the night. The innkeeper slipped into the room. He reached for the rope.

Nate sprang from his bed.

"Rope! Rope! Tie him up!" he said.

The rope slithered around the innkeeper's legs. It wrapped around his arms. It tied him up. The innkeeper could not move.

"Let me go!" the innkeeper said.

"After you give the tablecloth and the bank back," Nate said.

The innkeeper told Nate where the tablecloth and the bank were. Then Nate untied the innkeeper.

Nate gathered all his things and ran all the way home. He ran right into the cottage. He spread the tablecloth on the table. He put the piggy bank on the tablecloth.

"Mother! I got the North Wind's gifts back! Look!" he said. "Cloth! Cloth! Serve food! Bank! Bank! Make money!"

A pot of stew sprang up from the cloth. Coins spilled from the bank.

"Oh, my!" his mother said. "We will always have enough to eat. We will always have enough money."

Nate nodded.

"We also have the magic rope if anybody tries to trick us," he said.

He thought of the North Wind and smiled.

❧ Stone Soup ❧

Adapted by Lisa Harkrader ▪ Illustrated by Barbara Lanza

A traveling man walked along a dirt road. He had a feather in his hat. He had a smile on his face.

His name was Jack Grand, and he was a Rat-a-tat man. That meant he could do all sorts of things. He could tumble. He could dance. He could walk on his hands. He could yodel. He could hum. He could play the drum. He could sing. He could whittle. He even knew some riddles.

He could do many things. He had a good life. But sometimes, he went hungry. He was hungry now. He had not eaten in many days.

"There must be something to eat around here," he said. "A wild onion, some walnuts, or a dry old apple."

He searched the fields beside the road. He did not find anything to eat.

"Only rocks," he said.

He continued down the road. He walked up hills and through valleys. He walked and walked. He walked until he came to a village.

"Where there is a village, there are people. Where there are people, there is food. Maybe someone will feed a hungry traveling man," he said.

Jack ran to the village. He ran to the first house. A name was painted on the gate: TUBBS. He knocked on the door. An old man opened it. Jack swooped his hat from his head. He bowed low to the ground.

"May I help you?" asked the old man

"Hello, Mr. Tubbs," Jack said. "I'm Jack Grand, the Rat-a-tat Man. I can tumble. I can dance. I can walk on my hands."

"I am sorry," said Mr. Tubbs. "I have no money for a rat-a-tat man."

"I understand," Jack said. "The truth is, I'm hungry. I'll do a few tricks to pay for a meal."

"I have nothing to share," said Mr. Tubbs. "I have only a bit of salt and pepper. Ask Miss Grubbs next door."

Jack hurried to the next house. He knocked on the door.

A thin woman answered. Jack swooped his hat from his head. He bowed low to the ground.

"May I help you?" asked the thin woman.

"Hello, Miss Grubbs," he said. "I'm Jack Grand, the Rat-a-tat Man. I can yodel. I can hum. I can play the drum."

"I'm sorry," said Miss Grubbs. "I have no money for a rat-a-tat man."

"I understand," Jack said. "The truth is, I'm hungry. I'll do a few tricks to pay for a meal."

"I have nothing to share," said Miss Grubbs. "I have only a head of garlic. Ask Mrs. Chubbs next door."

Jack hurried to the next house. He knocked on the door.

A plump woman answered. Jack swooped his hat from his head. He bowed low to the ground.

"May I help you?" asked the plump woman.

"Hello, Mrs. Chubbs," Jack said. "I'm Jack Grand, the Rat-a-tat Man. I can sing. I can whittle. I can even tell some riddles."

"I'm sorry," said Mrs. Chubbs. "I have no money for a rat-a-tat man."

"I understand," Jack said. "The truth is, I'm hungry. I'll do a few tricks to pay for a meal."

"I have nothing to share," said Mrs. Chubbs. "I have only a few potatoes. Ask someone else."

Jack did. He knocked on every door in the village. He swooped his hat from his head. He bowed low to the ground.

Nobody had enough food to share.

One woman had only cabbage. Her neighbor had only a few carrots. One family had only some bacon. Another family had only a handful of beans.

Jack sighed and set off down the road. He walked for a long time. He no longer had a smile on his face. He was too hungry to smile. He decided to sit down and rest.

He saw a stone.

It was not like the other stones in the road. It was smooth and white and round. It gave Jack an idea.

He picked it up and examined it.

"Perfect," he said.

He was happy again. He was so happy he ran back to town. He knocked on the first door in the village. Mr. Tubbs answered.

"I know you have no food to share," Jack said. "Do you have a big pot I could borrow?"

"A big pot?" asked Mr. Tubbs.

Jack nodded. He held up the smooth, white stone.

"What have you got there?" asked Mr. Tubbs.

"It's a soup stone," Jack said.

"A soup stone?" asked Mr. Tubbs.

Jack nodded again.

"It makes great soup," he said. "I just add water."

Mr. Tubbs went inside. He came back with a big pot.

Jack carried the big pot to the village square. He filled it with water. He built a fire underneath it. He dropped the stone into it.

The pot bubbled and brewed. Jack waited and waited. He waited as long as he could. Then he dipped his spoon into the water. He tasted it.

"Perfect," he said.

"It's good?" asked Mr. Tubbs.

"Yes," said Jack. "It's very good. It would only be better if..."

Mr. Tubbs leaned in closer.

"If what?" he asked.

"Well," said Jack. "It would only be better with a little salt and pepper. Not much. Just a little. Oh, well. The soup will be just fine without it."

"Salt and pepper?" Mr. Tubbs asked.

"Yes," Jack said. "Don't worry, though. The soup will still be good."

"I have salt and pepper," said Mr. Tubbs.

"You do?" said Jack.

"Yes!" said Mr. Tubbs.

He ran to his cottage as fast as he could. He returned with a salt shaker and a pepper mill.

Jack sprinkled the salt into the pot. He ground the pepper into the pot. He stirred.

The pot bubbled and brewed. Jack waited and waited. He waited as long as he could. Then he dipped his spoon into the pot. He tasted the soup.

"Perfect," he said.

Miss Grubbs came out of her cottage. She had been watching Jack. She came over and peeked into the pot.

"It's stone soup," said Mr. Tubbs.

"Is it good?" asked Miss Grubbs.

"Yes," said Jack. "It's very good. It would only be better if…"

Miss Grubbs leaned in closer.

"If what?" she asked.

"Well," said Jack. "It would only be better with a little garlic. Not much. Just a little. Oh, well. The soup will be fine without it."

"Garlic?" Miss Grubbs asked.

"Yes," Jack said. "Don't worry, though. The soup will still be good."

"I have garlic," said Miss Grubbs.

"You do?" said Jack.

"Yes!" said Miss Grubbs.

She ran to her cottage as fast as she could. She returned with a beautiful head of garlic.

Jack chopped the head of garlic. He sprinkled the chopped garlic into the pot and stirred.

The pot bubbled and brewed. Jack waited and waited. He waited as long as he could. Then he dipped his spoon into the pot. He tasted the soup.

"Perfect," he said.

Mrs. Chubbs came out of her cottage. She had been watching Jack, too. She came over and peeked into the pot.

"It's stone soup," said Miss Grubbs.

"Is it good?" asked Mrs. Chubbs.

"Yes," said Jack. "It's very good. It would only be better if..."

Mrs. Chubbs leaned in closer.

"If what?" she asked.

"Well," said Jack. "It would only be better with a few potatoes. Not many. Just a few. Oh, well. The soup will be fine without them."

"Potatoes?" Mrs. Chubbs asked.

"Yes," Jack said. "Don't worry, though. The soup will still be good."

"I have potatoes," said Mrs. Chubbs.

"You do?" said Jack.

"Yes!" said Mrs. Chubbs.

She ran to her cottage as fast as she could. She returned with her apron full of potatoes.

Jack peeled and sliced the potatoes. He dropped the slices into the pot and stirred.

The pot bubbled and brewed. Jack waited and waited. He waited as long as he could. Then he dipped his spoon into the pot. He tasted the soup.

"Perfect," he said.

By this time, the entire village had gathered around Jack. They had been watching from their windows. They all wanted to know what was in the pot. They were very curious.

"It's stone soup," said Mrs. Chubbs.

"Is it good?" they asked.

"Yes," said Jack. "It's very good. It would only be better if we had . . ."

"If we had what?" asked the villagers.

"Cabbage," said Jack.

A woman ran to get cabbage.

"Carrots," said Jack.

A man ran to get carrots.

"A bit of bacon," said Jack, "and some beans."

The villagers ran to get the food. Jack threw it all into the pot and stirred. The pot bubbled and brewed. Jack could hardly wait. He dipped his spoon into the soup and tasted it.

"Perfect," he said.

"It's good?" everyone asked at once.

"Yes," said Jack, "and it's done."

Jack spooned soup out for everyone. He ate until he was full. All of the villagers ate until they were full. Everyone ate until the pot was empty.

Empty, that is, except for the smooth, white stone.

"Use it for your next pot of stone soup," Jack said to the villagers.

Then he did his tricks. He tumbled. He danced. He walked on his hands. He yodeled. He hummed. He played a drum. He sang. He whittled. He even told some riddles. When he was done, he waved to the villagers.

He walked for a while. Then he sat down to rest. He saw a rock. It was shiny and black. He picked it up and put it in his pocket.

"It's perfect," he said, "for making rock stew."

❧ Jack and the Beanstalk ❧

Adapted by Joanna Spathis ▪ Illustrated by Susan Spellman

J ack and his mother lived in a small country house. They were very poor. They did not have enough food to eat.

Jack's mother was sad. She remembered when there was plenty of food. They used to have a warm home. Jack used to have toys. Jack's father worked hard to give them things. But Jack's father was killed by a greedy giant. The giant stole everything they had.

"Son, you must go to town tomorrow," Jack's mother said. "It is time to sell our old cow."

The next morning, Jack led the cow into town.

"Your cow is just too skinny," the butcher said.

"Your cow is too old to milk," a farmer said.

No one wanted the cow. Then an old man walked up to Jack.

"What a perfect cow!" the old man said. "I will give you five beans for such a fine cow."

Jack looked at the five small beans and frowned.

"They are magic beans," the old man said. "Plant the beans. Your family will eat like royalty."

Jack skipped home with the five magic beans. He proudly showed his mother, but she only cried. She threw the beans into their dry garden. They went to bed hungry.

That night, the beans grew, and grew, and grew!

A beautiful beanstalk stood in the garden in the morning. The thick plant grew straight into the sky. Jack's mother picked lots of plump beans.

"We will have a wonderful bean soup," she said.

Jack had other ideas. He wanted to climb the tall beanstalk into the clouds. He put one foot on the beanstalk and pulled himself up.

"Be careful," Jack's mother said, "and don't be late for supper!"

Jack climbed and climbed. The houses of the town looked small when he looked down. They were as small as toys. He climbed some more.

"I just want to touch a cloud," he thought.

As he climbed through the clouds, Jack saw a castle. He rubbed his eyes. The castle was huge. It was bigger than anything he had ever imagined. The road to the castle was paved in gold.

"I am so cold and thirsty!" Jack thought. "I will go to the castle."

Jack knocked at the door. He knocked again and again. The heavy door finally opened. A very tall woman looked around. She did not see Jack because he was so small.

"Hello!" Jack yelled. "Down here!"

"Oh, my! Look what we have here," the tall woman said.

"I am very cold and thirsty," Jack said.

"Please come inside," the tall woman said.

She gently picked Jack up and took him inside.

She bundled Jack in her handkerchief. She gave him a thimble of tea.

"You must be very quiet," she said. "My husband has a terrible temper. A very terrible temper. He is a giant, you know."

Jack gasped. He knew all about the giant. He was very frightened.

Suddenly, Jack felt the floor shake. A cake in the oven fell. Jack heard loud footsteps. He hid behind a bowl of fruit on the table.

"Fee-fi-fo-fum! I smell a little boy!" the giant yelled.

"Don't be silly," the giant's wife said. "It's just your supper that you smell. Sit and eat."

The giant's wife placed a large plate of food on the table.

The giant ate his supper in two huge swallows. He ate a whole loaf of bread. He wiped his beard on his sleeve when he was finished.

"Bring me my hen," the giant said.

The giant's wife brought in a hen. Jack could not believe his eyes. The magic hen had belonged to his father. Jack knew it laid eggs of pure gold.

Jack watched as the hen laid her eggs. The giant laughed and demanded more eggs. Jack was no longer afraid. He was angry.

The giant finally had enough eggs. He leaned back in his chair and fell asleep. He snored loudly.

Jack jumped from the table. He grabbed the hen and ran from the castle. He climbed down the beanstalk as fast as he could.

Jack's mother was waiting for him when he arrived.

"I was worried," his mother said. "Your bean soup is cold."

Jack proudly held out the magic hen.

"Our hen!" Jack's mother said. "How wonderful!"

The magic hen laid golden eggs every morning. Jack and his mother had plenty to eat. They shared their good fortune with all of their neighbors. But Jack was not satisfied. He decided to climb up the beanstalk again.

"You must be very careful," Jack's mother said.

"I promise to be careful," he said.

He hugged his mother and went to the giant's castle.

This time he did not knock at the door. He quietly crept into the castle. The giant's wife was making a stew. Jack hid in the sugar bowl.

Suddenly, Jack heard the familiar footsteps. The salt shaker toppled over. Jack held on as the sugar bowl shook.

"Fee-fi-fo-fum! I smell a little boy!" the giant yelled.

"We are alone," the giant's wife said. "What would a little boy be doing here? You are just upset because you lost your hen."

The giant ate his stew. Then he called to his wife.

"Bring me my bags of gold!" he yelled.

"I will bring you your gold," his wife said. "There is no need to shout."

Jack giggled and peeked out of the sugar bowl.

Jack watched the giant count his bags of coins. Jack knew the coins had belonged to his father. Jack became angrier and angrier at the ugly giant.

The giant soon grew tired of counting. His head fell on the table with a loud thump. He began to snore.

The giant's snore shook the whole kitchen. Jack jumped out of the sugar bowl. He ran across the table. He grabbed a bag of coins. He climbed down from the table and ran.

He ran and ran. He ran as fast as his legs could carry him. He ran for the beanstalk. He climbed through the clouds and found his way home.

His mother was waiting for him.

"Jack, you are late again," she said. "I was very worried. I made a nice stew for you. It is cold now."

"I have another surprise for you," Jack said.

Jack handed his mother the bag of coins.

"Jack!" his mother said. "It is a miracle! We have more than we need now. It is time to cut down the beanstalk."

"Not yet," Jack said. "We do not have everything yet."

"We do," she said. "We have plenty for our neighbors as well."

"Tomorrow, I will climb one last time," Jack said.

"One last time," she said. "Then I will cut it down myself."

"Okay," Jack said. "It will be my last climb."

In the morning, Jack climbed the beanstalk again. He climbed his way through the clouds.

He walked up the gold road to the castle. The giant's wife had left the kitchen window open. Jack climbed through it. He hid behind a heavy curtain.

The giant's wife hummed softly. Jack waited patiently.

Suddenly, Jack heard the giant's footsteps. The windows shook. A teacup fell off the table. All the curtains swayed.

"Could you please walk more softly?" the giant's wife asked.

The giant sniffed at the air.

"Fee-fi-fo-fum! I smell a little boy!" the giant yelled.

The giant's wife checked behind the bowl of fruit. She looked in the sugar bowl. She did not see a little boy.

"You smell these meat pies," she said. "It is time to eat."

The giant ate the six meat pies in six bites.

"Bring me my harp," the giant said.

Jack knew the harp belonged to his father. Jack's mother had told him stories about it. It was a magic harp. It had the most beautiful sound.

"Play," the giant said.

The harp played. The giant's eyes grew heavy. He started to snore. The snoring blew the curtains back.

Jack climbed onto the table. He grabbed the harp.

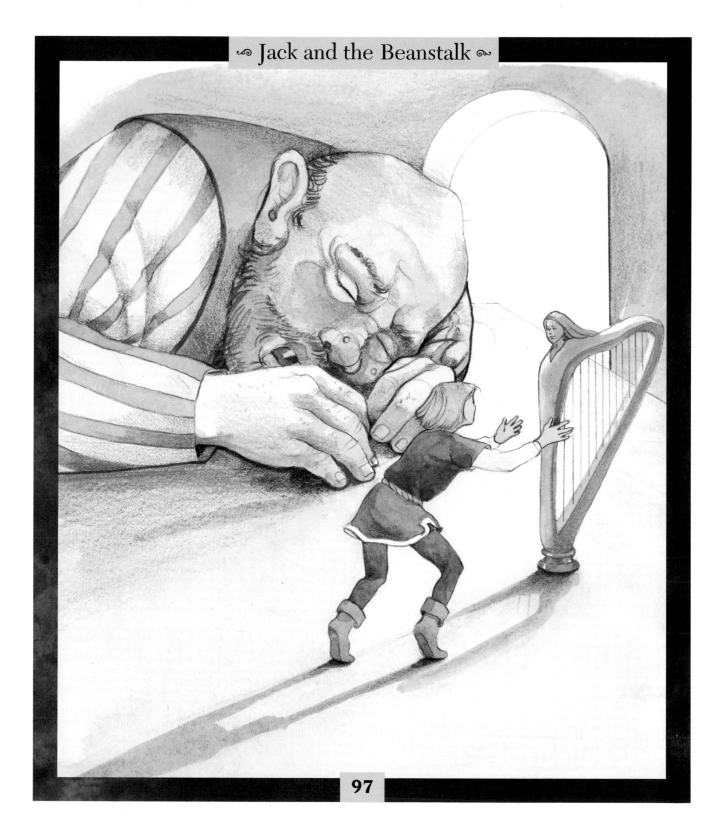

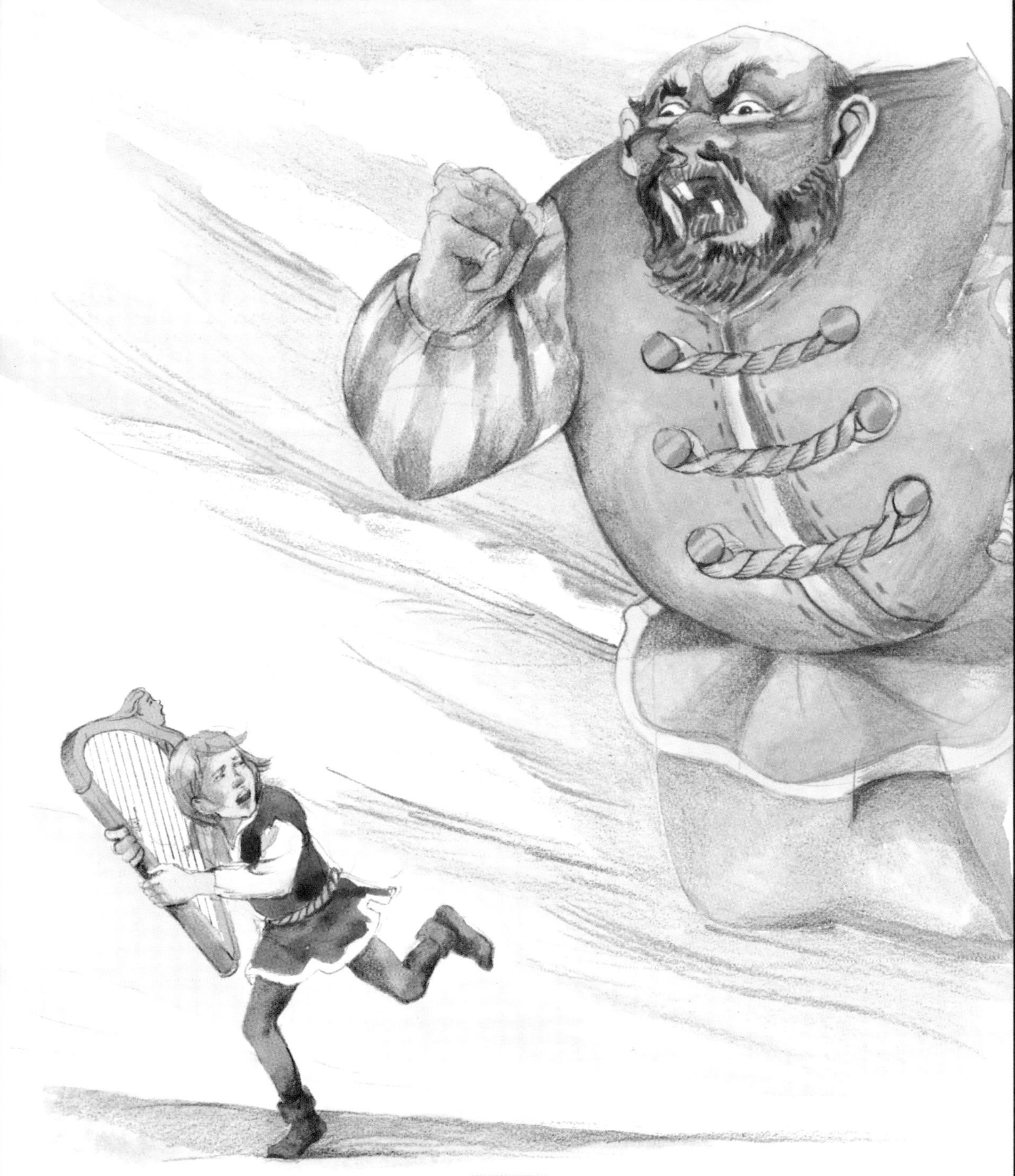

The harp shrieked. It was not used to being interrupted. The shrieks woke the giant. The giant yelled as he rose from the table.

"Why are you raising your voice?" the giant's wife asked.

"That boy has my harp!" the giant yelled.

Jack jumped from the table. He ran with the harp. He ran beneath the table. He ran between the chairs.

The giant smashed the table with his heavy fists. He pushed the chairs aside. He tried to grab Jack.

Jack was too quick. He jumped through the open window. He ran down the golden road. He ran and ran. He ran faster than he ever had before.

"Come back with my harp!" the giant yelled.

The giant took huge steps, but he was still slow. He had trouble seeing Jack, because Jack was so small. The giant's footsteps shook the clouds and made it rain.

Jack finally reached the beanstalk. He climbed down as quickly as he could. The giant was close behind him. The giant shook the beanstalk. Jack held on as it swayed back and forth.

Jack could see his mother on the ground. He was late again!

"I made you a warm supper. It is cold now!" his mother said.

Jack jumped off the beanstalk.

"I will cut the beanstalk down," she said. "I told you I would."

Jack's mother was very upset. She did not know the giant was climbing down the beanstalk.

"Mother, chop it down!" Jack said.

"I will, then," she said. "I told you to be careful. You came down the beanstalk much too fast."

"Hurry, Mother!" Jack said.

Jack pointed towards the sky.

His mother looked up into the clouds. She saw the beanstalk swaying. Then she saw a giant pair of boots!

She struck the beanstalk with an axe. It began to fall over.

The magic beanstalk crashed to the ground. The giant crashed down with the beanstalk.

Jack and his mother celebrated with all their neighbors. They had a great feast. They danced to the lovely songs of the harp.

Jack walked to town the next morning. He bought his mother a healthy new cow.

"Son, I am proud of you," his mother said.

She was happy again. That made Jack happy, too.

They lived happily. They had plenty to eat. Their home was warm and cozy. Jack had toys again.

They would not see the giant ever again.

❧ Rip Van Winkle ❧

Adapted by Brian Conway ▪ Illustrated by John Lund

The Catskill Mountains are a magical place. They are a wild place. They are a place filled with many beautiful sights. Clear brooks run down the hills. Valleys spread out wide. Stone cliffs rise up to the sky. Tall trees reach into the clouds.

The mountains are filled with legends, too. The mountain people tell the legends like amazing stories. The stories seem too strange to be true. One can never be sure.

One story might be true. It is about a man named Rip Van Winkle.

Rip lived in a town in the foothills. He was a friendly man. He always had a smile for anyone he met. He greeted everybody with a wave and a tip of his hat. Everyone loved him.

The children in town especially loved him. They followed him wherever he went.

"Give us piggyback rides, Mr. Van Winkle," they said.

Rip always did. He played games with them, too. He flew kites with them. He shot marbles with them. He even jumped rope with them.

Even the neighborhood dogs loved Rip. They never barked when he passed by. They wagged their tails when he petted them.

Rip Van Winkle was a wonderful neighbor. He could never turn down a neighbor who asked for help. He always helped his neighbors with their chores. He loved to help.

Rip had just one fault. He did not like to do his chores.

He helped his neighbors with their chores. He loved to help. He just did not like to do his own chores.

That made everyone happy except his wife.

His fences always fell over. The weeds in his yard always grew fast and wild. His cow was always running away. His pigs were always trampling through the garden.

Rip's children were as raggedy as his farm. Their clothes were always torn. Their faces were always dirty. They ran around without shoes. They did not like to do their chores either.

Young Rip was the worst of all. He never listened to anybody. He never did what was asked of him. He was just like his father.

"Young Rip is going to turn out just like his father," the neighbors said.

Rip's wife was never very happy with either of them.

"I thought you were going to fix the fence today," she said.

"It's a very big fence," Rip said.

"Get Young Rip to help you," she said.

Rip called for his son, but Young Rip did not come.

He decided to leave the fence until tomorrow morning. He called for his dog, Wolf. He waved to his daughter, Judith.

He headed for the mountains.

Rip and his dog spent a lot of time in the mountains. Rip liked to go fishing. Wolf liked to hunt for squirrels.

Some days, they just walked.

"I have had a busy day," Rip said.

Wolf wagged his tail.

"Let's find a place where there are no fences around," he said.

They walked up one of the tall mountains. Halfway up, Rip sat down and enjoyed the view. Wolf sat next to him.

Rip and Wolf passed the whole afternoon that way.

"It's getting late," Rip said. "We should get home."

Rip stood up. He heard someone call his name. He did not see anyone. There was no one around.

"Rip Van Winkle," a voice said.

Rip turned around. He saw a strange little man. He carried a huge barrel on his shoulder.

"Would you help me with this?" the little man asked.

The little man was strange. But Rip could not refuse anyone who asked for help.

"Of course," Rip said. "I would love to help."

Rip took the barrel from the strange little man. Rip climbed up the mountain after him.

Rip heard loud claps and crashes as they climbed. It sounded just like thunder. Rip looked around. There was not a cloud in the sky.

"There must be a storm on the other side of the mountain," Rip said.

The little man just smiled. He led Rip and Wolf through a crack in a cliff. There was a clearing inside.

There was a group in the clearing. Many strange little men were gathered there. Rip stared at them.

"I have lived in these mountains all my life," he thought. "I have never seen such strange little men before."

Rip saw something even more unusual as they got closer. The strange little men were bowling.

Every time the ball hit the pins, there was a crash. The sound echoed through the mountains. It sounded like thunder!

The little men stopped bowling when they saw Rip and Wolf.

"Thank you, neighbor," one strange little man said.

He took the barrel from Rip. He poured a dark liquid from it. The strange little men passed around cups and drank.

They offered a cup to Rip. He drank the dark liquid. It was very tasty. He asked for more.

He drank several cups and started to feel tired. His eyes drooped. His head felt heavy. He drifted off to sleep.

It was late when Rip woke up. The sun was shining high in the sky. It was almost the afternoon.

He was no longer in the clearing. He was back where he had met the first little man.

"I have been here all night," he said. "Mrs. Van Winkle is going to be very upset with me."

He whistled for his dog. Wolf did not come running.

"Maybe Wolf ran home," he said. "I should do the same thing."

Rip's knees cracked when he stood up. His legs were stiff.

"Sleeping outside isn't good for me," he said. "My legs feel like they belong to an old man."

He started down the hill.

He had dreamed about strange little men. He remembered his dream as he walked. The dream had seemed so real. He felt confused.

Rip walked into town. The people he saw did not look familiar. He did not know anyone. They did not seem to know him.

The townspeople stared at Rip. He smiled. He waved. He tipped his hat. Some of the people laughed. Others looked the other way.

Finally, Rip looked down. He saw why everyone had been staring at him. He had a long gray beard!

Now, reality seemed like a dream.

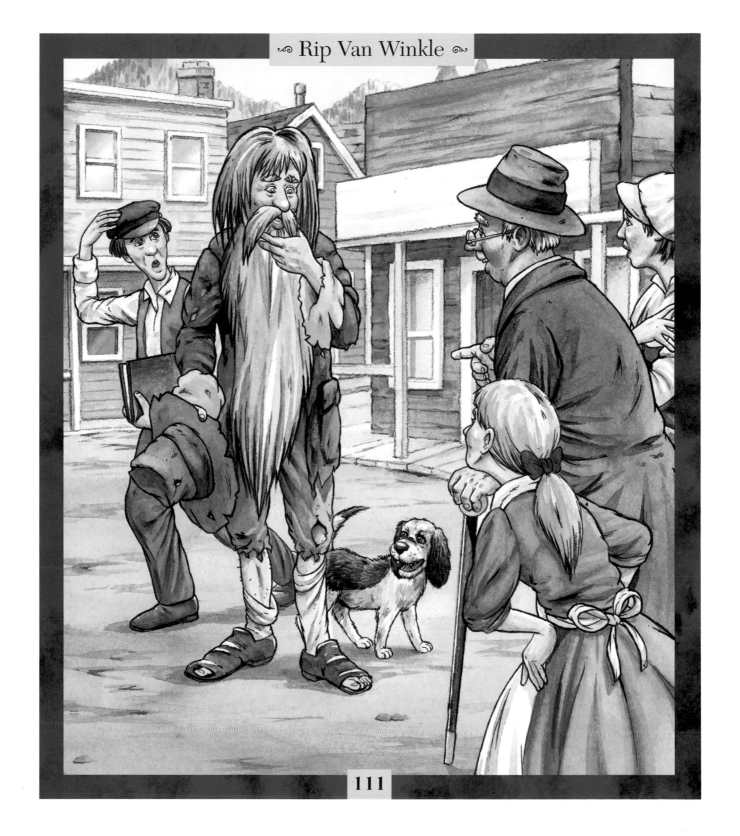

Rip's beard had grown down to his knees. It was gray and white. It was knotted and tangled.

His clothes were ripped and tattered. He was dirty. He looked like a crazy old man.

Children raced up to Rip.

"Who are you, old man?" one boy asked.

"What are you doing in our town?" asked another.

Rip was more confused than ever.

He walked through town. The people were different. The buildings were different. The dogs ran after him and barked.

"I'd better get home," Rip said. "Things will be all right once I see my wife and children."

But Rip got lost on the way to his house. The paths and roads were no longer the same.

After some time, Rip found his farmhouse. It did not look at all like it did the day before. The fence had fallen to the ground. Weeds grew all over. The roof was falling in. The front door was swinging on its hinges.

Rip waited for his wife and children to appear. No one moved around the house. No one came out. The swinging door creaked in the breeze.

Rip walked slowly toward the house. It was dark and dirty inside. Nobody had lived there in a very long time.

Rip ran back to town. He wanted to find something familiar. He wanted to find someone who remembered him.

He thought he could find his friends at the inn. But the inn was not where it used to be. There was a schoolhouse there instead.

A man dressed in a fine suit walked up to Rip.

"What are you doing here?" he asked.

"I am looking for someone who remembers me," Rip said.

"Did you used to live around here?" the man asked.

Rip did not know what to say.

"I asked you a question," the man said.

"I know," Rip said. "I just don't know how to answer."

"It's a simple question," the man said. "Did you used to live here?"

"Yes," Rip said. "I lived here yesterday."

"I don't know what you are up to," the man said.

"I'm not trying to start a fight," Rip said. "I am a kind person. My name is Rip Van Winkle."

"Rip Van Winkle?" the man asked. "I know Rip, and you're not him. That's Rip Van Winkle over there."

The man pointed to a tree in the park. There was a young man standing under it.

He looked like Rip had looked yesterday.

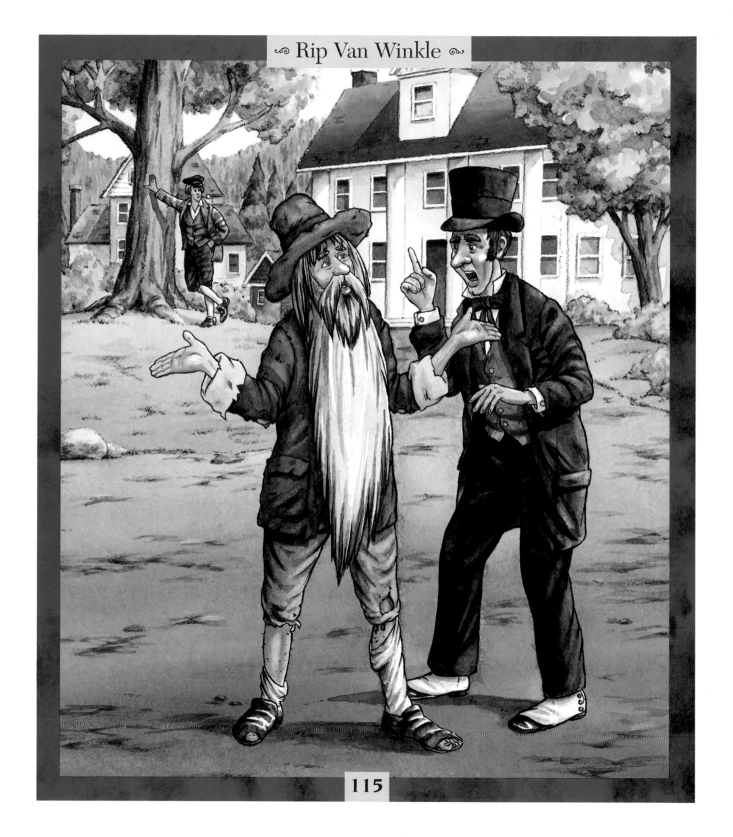

Then a woman and her family wanted to meet the old, bearded stranger.

"Hello," the woman said. "I am Judith Gardener. These are my children."

"What is your father's name?" he asked.

"Rip Van Winkle was his name," she said. "I have not seen him in twenty years." Tears sprang from her eyes.

"And what about your mother?" Rip asked.

"She passed away a few months ago," Judith said.

"Don't you recognize me?" he asked. "I am your father!"

Young Rip and Judith did not believe Rip's story.

"I fell asleep on the mountain," he said.

Young Rip liked to help. He went to find the tailor's wife. She was the oldest woman in town. If she did not know the stranger, nobody would.

The old woman looked into old Rip's eyes. She squinted. "Sure enough," she said. "Welcome home, Rip Van Winkle."

The whole town gathered to hear Rip's story.

He told the people about the little men's game. He told them about the strange liquid he drank. He told them about his very long nap.

Everyone was glad to have old Rip Van Winkle back.

His story became a legend. Whenever people hear the sound of thunder on the Catskill Mountains they talk. They say it is Rip's strange little friends bowling on the mountaintops.

❧ The Selfish Giant ❧

Adapted by Lisa Harkrader ▪ Illustrated by Tammie Lyon

acob ran behind his friends. His feet crunched through fallen leaves. His schoolbooks jostled in his arms.

"Wait for me," he called.

He raced to catch up with Matthew and Rachel. They were taking him to the castle on the hill. He had never been there before.

They stopped at the edge of town. Jacob looked up. The castle towered above them. It was big and gray and gloomy.

It was also empty. The windows were dark. The doors were bolted shut. Nobody lived there. The owner had been away for many years. He had been away for so long nobody remembered him.

But Jacob was not afraid of the old, gloomy castle. The lovely garden surrounding it was wonderful.

Late summer sun shone over the green grass. Butterflies flitted from flower to flower. Birds twittered in the trees. The leaves of the trees ruffled in the breeze.

Jacob, Matthew, and Rachel tossed their jackets and schoolbooks in the grass. Matthew and Rachel ran through the garden, playing tag.

Jacob did not want to play tag. He saw a tree in the corner of the garden. Hanging from each branch were ripe golden peaches.

He ran to the tree. He stretched. He jumped. He tried to reach a peach.

"What do you think you're doing?" a booming voice asked.

Jacob turned around. An enormous man was standing inside the gate. He was a giant! His legs were like tree trunks. His feet were like boats. His chest was like a barrel. He was so tall his head brushed the tallest branches. He was so strong the ground shook when he walked.

He was very angry.

"Get out of my garden!" he yelled.

"Yes, sir!" Matthew and Rachel said.

Matthew and Rachel scrambled through the grass. They grabbed their jackets and schoolbooks. They ran past the giant. They went through the gate. They ran from the garden.

Jacob just stared at the giant.

"Your garden?" he asked. "Nobody lives here."

The giant stared back.

"I live here. I went away. I'm back. This is my castle and my garden. I don't need wild children ruining it."

"We are not ruining anything," Jacob said. "We are not wild. It is just so wonderful here. We were just playing."

"It's mine!" yelled the giant. "Get out!"

"You're just, you're just . . . selfish!" Jacob said.

He snatched his jacket and schoolbooks from the grass. He looked at the giant for a minute. Then he ran from the garden.

Jacob, Matthew, and Rachel stayed far away from the castle after that. Autumn turned to winter, and winter turned to spring. Jacob and his friends played in the schoolyard. They played in the park. They played in their own yards at home.

It was not the same.

"It's not like playing in the castle garden," Jacob said.

"Maybe the giant will go away again," Matthew said.

"Maybe he's already gone," Rachel said.

"We should go and look," Jacob said. "He can't be mad at us for looking."

Jacob and his friends ran to the castle. It was still big and gray and gloomy. The windows were still dark.

But they could no longer see the garden. The giant had built a stone wall around it. On the wall was a sign. It read:

KEEP OUT!

ESPECIALLY CHILDREN

"The giant is still here," Matthew said.

"It doesn't look like he'll ever go away," Rachel said.

"Let's look over the wall," Jacob said.

A pile of firewood was stacked against the wall. They climbed onto it and peeked over the wall.

What they saw made them gasp.

"Oh, no!" said Jacob.

They stared at the garden.

Snow covered the grass. A cold wind whistled. The trees were bare. The branches stood crooked and black against the sky.

Jacob shook his head.

"What happened?" he asked. "Why hasn't winter gone from the garden? Why hasn't spring come?"

"Maybe it's just taking longer this year," Matthew said.

"Maybe the flowers will start to bloom soon," Rachel said.

Each day, Jacob, Matthew, and Rachel ran to the castle. Each day, they stood on the pile of firewood. Each day, they peeked over the wall. Each day, Jacob shook his head.

Outside of the garden, the days were becoming warmer. The sun was brighter. Flowers blossomed. Spring was turning to summer.

Inside of the garden, it was still winter. The flowers were not blossoming. The trees were not budding. Birds no longer twittered in the trees. Butterflies no longer flitted around.

Only one lone peach still hung on the peach tree. The other peaches had fallen to the ground. They poked up through the snow. They were shriveled and brown.

"It is no longer wonderful," Jacob said.

Jacob, Matthew, and Rachel kept watching the garden. Each day, it was the same. It was always winter.

One day, they saw the giant. He was leaning over a rosebush. A tiny rosebud was starting to bloom.

"Look!" Jacob said. "A flower."

"Maybe spring is finally coming to the garden," said Rachel.

The giant looked at the flower for a long time. He reached down to touch it. Its petals crumbled and fell to the ground.

The giant sighed and shook his head. He was still big. He was still strong. But he did not look angry anymore.

"He looks lonely," Jacob said.

"He should be lonely," Rachel said.

"He yelled at us," Matthew said.

"And chased us away," Rachel said.

"He just looks so sad," Jacob said. "We should help him."

"I'm not going to help him," Matthew said.

"I'm not going to help him, either," Rachel said.

Jacob watched the giant. The giant stared at his dead garden. He stared at the wilted flower and bare trees. He shook his head. He turned and went back into his castle.

"I'd help you," Jacob whispered, "if only I knew how."

Matthew and Rachel climbed down from the stack of firewood.

Jacob felt so sad. He took one last look at the garden. He turned to climb down, too.

He lost his balance. His foot slipped, and the firewood began to tumble down. He kicked at the wall. He tried to regain his balance. One of the stones moved when he kicked it.

"Look," said Jacob. "It's loose!"

Matthew and Rachel helped him move the stone. They wiggled it. They pushed it. They pulled it. They tugged it. The stone finally broke free with a loud pop.

All of them tumbled backward in the grass. They stared at the stone. They stared at the hole where the stone had been. The hole went all the way through the wall. It went all the way through to the garden!

"Should we go through?" Matthew asked.

"Yes," Rachel said. "Unless you're afraid."

"I'm not afraid," Matthew said. "Are you afraid?"

"I'm not afraid," said Rachel. "Are you afraid, Jacob?"

"No," Jacob said. "I'm not afraid."

"Good," said Rachel. "You can go first, then."

Jacob swallowed. He looked into the hole. He climbed into it. He crawled all the way through to the other side.

Jacob stepped into the garden. Matthew and Rachel followed.

Wind whistled through the trees. Snow swirled at their feet. Their breath came out in little white puffs. They shivered. They felt very sad.

"Maybe we should go back," Matthew said.

"The giant will yell at us again," Rachel said.

"I don't think he will," Jacob said.

"He will yell at us," Matthew said.

"We ruined his garden wall," Rachel said.

"No, he won't," Jacob said. "We'll stay here in the corner by the peach tree. The giant won't even see us. The tree limbs will hide us."

"Okay," Matthew said.

"But only for a little while," Rachel said.

Matthew and Rachel ran to make snow angels.

Jacob did not want to make snow angels. He stared at the peach tree. He stared at the lone peach. It hung from the highest branch.

He stretched. He jumped. He tried to reach the peach.

"You'll never get it like that," said a booming voice.

A huge hand picked him up from the ground. It lifted him to the highest branch of the tree.

Jacob turned around. He was staring right straight into the eyes of the selfish giant.

"Oh!" said Jacob.

The giant smiled at him.

The giant lifted Jacob to the top of the tree. He held Jacob steady. Jacob reached up. He plucked the peach from the highest branch.

"Thank you," Jacob whispered.

"No," said the giant. "Thank you."

The giant pointed to the peach tree. New buds were popped out on the branches. They turned into leaves.

Jacob stared at them. He turned and stared at the garden.

The snow had melted where Rachel and Matthew were playing. Green grass grew beneath their feet. The sun broke through the clouds. Butterflies flitted across the grass. Birds twittered in the trees. Flowers popped up all over the garden.

"Spring has finally come!" Jacob said.

"Yes," the giant said. "You brought it. You brought joy to the garden and to me. The joy brought back the spring."

Jacob, Matthew, and Rachel went to the garden every day after that. They taught the giant to play tag. The giant lifted them up to pick peaches. They ate the peaches and chased the butterflies.

Summer came to the garden and then autumn and winter. But winter did not stay. The snow melted. The sun shone. Each year, spring returned.

❧ The Little Dutch Boy ❧

Adapted by Brian Conway ▪ Illustrated by Linda Dockey Graves

*O*nce there was a little Dutch boy named Hans. He lived with his mother in a little town in Holland.

Holland is a very flat country. The town Hans lived in was by the sea. The farmers who lived there built big walls around their farms. The big walls, called dikes, kept the sea from flooding the farms.

Hans was a regular boy. He went to school with the other children in town. He played with his friends after school. He did his chores. He helped his mother whenever he could.

"Hans," his mother said. "I need you to take this basket of food to Mr. Van Notten."

Mr. Van Notten was an old friend of theirs. He lived on a farm on the edge of town. It was a long way to his house. The walk there and back always took most of the day.

"I wanted to go fishing," Hans said.

"You can fish tomorrow," his mother said. "Mr. Van Notten is waiting for you. Now, Mr. Van Notten always asks you to stay for dinner. What will you tell him?"

"I will thank him," Hans said. "But I will tell him I have to get home. It is a long walk."

"You are a good boy, Hans," his mother said. "I will have dinner waiting for you when you return."

Hans set off on the main road out of town. The dike was built alongside of the road. He tapped the dike with a stick as he walked. He thought about his friends. They were fishing at the beach.

He thought of Mr. Van Notten. Mr. Van Notten was an old man. He lived alone. He had only his old dog to keep him company. He was always very happy to have visitors.

"My dear friend!" Mr. Van Notten said. "I am so glad to see you!"

Hans smiled and shook Mr. Van Notten's hand. He gave Mr. Van Notten the big basket of food.

"Look at all of these wonderful things," Mr. Van Notten said. "Come inside. We will have a bite to eat."

Hans knew he had to start for home. But he was very thirsty after his long walk. Mr. Van Notten had hot cocoa warming on the fire.

"I can only stay for a cup of cocoa," he said.

Hans stayed for a cup of cocoa. He also stayed for a few stories.

Mr. Van Notten told the best stories.

Hans lost track of time. He looked out the window. Hans saw it was already beginning to get dark outside.

"Oh, no! It's getting dark," Hans said. "I must be getting home."

"It looks like a storm is coming," Mr. Van Notten said. "Hurry home. Be very careful if it starts to rain."

Hans walked up the road. He felt a few cold raindrops fall. The wind began to blow. The sky became very dark and stormy.

Hans pulled his hat down over his ears. The raindrops turned into sheets of rain. Every gust of cold wind made him walk faster. The storm got worse with every step.

The strong wind made the trees bend low. It blew the cold rain into his eyes. He walked into the wind. He slipped and slid along the muddy road.

He could not walk very fast.

The wind knocked him back. It spun him around.

The rain was really bad. He could hardly see a thing in front of him.

"I hope this is the right direction," he said to himself.

He looked down at the mud at his feet.

"I hope I am still walking on the road," he thought.

Hans came around a corner in the road. The winds let up just a little. He lifted his head and saw the dike in front of him.

"Thank goodness," he said. "I am almost home."

He went over to the dike. He would use it to lead him back home.

But something about the dike was not right. It was raining hard, but there was even more water. Seawater gushed from the stones. There was a crack in the wall.

The dike had sprung a leak!

Hans ran towards town. He felt his way along the dike through the storm. He hurried as fast as he could go.

"I must get to town and warn the others," he thought.

Hans never thought the dike could break. It was the strongest thing he knew. It was older than any building in town.

The dike had stood up to many fierce storms. Strong winds and crashing waves had never harmed it. The dike kept the little town safe.

But Hans had never seen a storm like this one before. The old stone wall was no match. The winds and waves were stronger. If the dike broke, the town would be washed away by the sea.

Hans arrived in town at last. The streets were dark and empty.

"The dike is leaking!" he shouted.

There was terrible thunder and howling winds.

"We must fix the dike!" he shouted.

No one could hear him.

"We are in danger!" he shouted.

His voice was nothing more than a squeak. The storm was too loud.

Hans did not see anyone. Every house was closed up. Every door was bolted shut. Every window was sealed and shuttered.

"Somebody help!" Hans shouted.

Nobody heard him.

Hans thought of the dike. He thought of the crack in the stones. He was the only person who knew the town was in danger.

"There is no one to help me," he thought. "I will just have to think of something. I will have to fix the dike."

Hans knew nothing about mending walls. He had no tools. He ran back to the crack in the dike anyway.

The crack had grown bigger!

He looked around for something to cover the crack.

He found some branches. He put them into the crack. The seawater squirted around them.

He dug up a handful of mud. He put it into the crack. The seawater washed it away.

Hans was scared. He could hear waves pounding against the stone wall. The crack in the dike became a little bigger with every crash. The storm was not settling down. It was getting worse.

"I have to do something," he thought.

There was nothing left to plug the hole. Hans balled up his fist. He pushed it into the hole. The steady stream of cold water around it slowed down. The wall only dripped.

He had plugged up the hole. He was glad he had thought of something. But he was worried too. How long could he hold back the sea?

He tried not to think about that. He tried to be proud of his cleverness. He tried to feel strong as he held back the sea.

He knew his mother was worrying about him. He hoped she would send someone to look for him.

Moments became hours. The rain and winds became colder. No one came looking for him.

"No one will venture out in this storm," Hans thought.

He was still very scared. He was also very tired.

He was soaked through. His legs were shaking in a muddy puddle. His arm ached as he continued to push it into the wall. His hand was frozen. He could hardly feel it.

"I must save the town," he said over and over again. "I must save the town. I must save the town."

Hans's mother was very worried. She had been waiting for Hans for a very long time.

She opened her shutter to look out the window. The shutter snapped back. Wind and rain blew in.

"Oh, Hans," she said, "where are you?"

She closed the window. She hoped that Hans had kept out of the storm. She hoped he had stayed in the safety of Mr. Van Notten's house. No one could survive outside during such a storm.

The storm settled down the next morning. Hans did not notice when the sun came up. He shivered with cold. His legs were exhausted.

He could no longer feel his hand. He had not let it drop from the wall. He still held back the rough morning tide.

Mr. Van Notten had worried all night about Hans. He wondered if Hans had made it home. He wanted to be sure. He called for his old dog. They walked towards town.

Mr. Van Notten walked towards the dike. He squinted and saw a familiar shape. When he got closer, he saw that it was Hans. His dear friend was holding back the sea with his little hand.

Hans sniffled and yawned. He shivered and shook. He did not hear Mr. Van Notten calling to him.

"My dear friend!" Mr. Van Notten said. "You are a hero. You've saved the town from a flood."

Hans looked up with a small smile.

"I must save the town," he said.

"You have saved the town," Mr. Van Notten said. "Hold on just a little while longer."

Mr. Van Notten hurried up the road to get help. The townspeople were just waking up. A group of people soon arrived at the dike. They brought tools and supplies to repair the dike. They brought dry blankets for Hans

They carried him home to his mother. She was very happy to see him. She warmed his face with kisses. She held his worn fingers and rubbed his stiff legs. She fed him hot soup.

The doctor arrived to check on Hans. Hans was tucked into his warm, dry bed. He had the sniffles, but he was okay.

He was not scared anymore. He was safe.

"My brave little boy," his mother said. "You saved us all."

"I don't think I will go fishing today after all," Hans said.

Everyone heard about what Hans had done. They were proud of him.

"That one little boy saved our whole town," said the shoemaker.

"He held back the sea with just one hand," said the baker.

The mayor called all the townspeople together.

"Hans worked through the night to hold back the flood," he said. "He saved us all while we were asleep. While he is sleeping, we must prepare a celebration for him."

Hans woke up to the sound of a band playing. Hans peeked out of his bedroom window. He saw every face in town in the street below. All the faces looked up at him and cheered.

The mayor presented Hans with a medal of honor. The little Dutch boy was a hero. Even after Hans was all grown up, everyone still called him the boy who saved the town.

Ali Baba

Adapted by Jennifer Boudart ▪ Illustrated by Anthony Lewis

n ancient times, there was a man named Ali Baba. He lived in Persia. He was a woodcutter. He thought he would always be a woodcutter.

But that changed one day.

One day, Ali Baba was working in the forest. He climbed a tree to cut a high branch. He stopped chopping when he heard the sound of hoofbeats.

A group of riders came. They did not look like friendly men to Ali Baba. They looked like thieves.

They rode beneath his tree. He counted them as they passed. There were forty riders. The number made him think. A band of forty thieves traveled around Persia. They stole anything and everything. They did not mind hurting people to do it.

The men stopped their horses near a rock wall. Each rider pulled a heavy bag from his saddle.

"Open sesame!" the leader said.

A door opened in the rocks.

Ali Baba watched the men go inside. When they came back, they did not have the bags. They had left the bags inside.

The captain came out last.

"Close sesame!" he said.

The rock door shut tight.

Ali Baba watched the men ride away. He knew it was the famous band of thieves. No one knew where the band had its hideout. He had just found it. He climbed down and stood before the wall.

"Open sesame!" he said.

The door opened.

Ali Baba put down his axe and went inside.

There was not much light in the cave. He took a step inside. He squinted his eyes to see better. The floor was covered with coins!

He began to search the cave. It was filled with riches. There were colorful rugs, silver bowls, gold bars, and shiny jewels. He also found the bags of coins the thieves had brought. He grabbed all the bags he could carry.

"Close sesame!" he said.

The door shut tight.

Ali Baba raced home in his wagon. When his wife saw the coins, she was shocked. She was also scared.

"Did you break the law or hurt anyone?" she asked.

"No. This money came from the thieves," he said. "They have hurt many people. We must use it for good."

He told her about the thieves and their hideout. He told her about all the things they had left behind. He did not realize he had left something behind, too. He left his axe on the ground inside the cave.

Ali Baba used the money for good. He moved his family into a better house. He opened a shop. The shop was filled with fine goods at fair prices. It was soon a busy place.

The forty thieves were busy, too. It was a long time before they returned to their hideout.

"Open sesame!" the captain said.

The door opened. When it did, something on the ground caught his eye. It was an axe. The axe did not belong to any of his men. They carried knives. They had not stolen it. It was worthless. The thieves ran into the cave. They had been robbed!

The captain went to the smartest man in his band.

"Go to town," he said. "Find a poor man who is newly rich. Get his name. We will get even with him!"

The man went to town. He dressed like a trader. The first shop he visited belonged to Ali Baba. Morgiana was working for Ali Baba that day. She was a good worker and a good friend.

"I am a trader," the man said. "I have never seen this shop before."

"It is new," she said. "It belongs to Ali Baba."

"Interesting," the man said.

"He is not trading right now though," she said.

Morgiana did not like the way the trader looked.

"Too bad," the man said. "Does Ali Baba own any other shops?"

"This is the only one," she said. "He just got the money to open it."

The trader thanked Morgiana and smiled. She did not like that smile.

The man went back to his captain.

"I have a name. It's Ali Baba," he said. "He just got some money. He opened a shop. He lives the life of a rich man."

The captain gave the thief a piece of white chalk.

"Return to Ali Baba's shop. Mark an **X** on the door so we will know it. We will break into the shop and teach Ali Baba a lesson," the captain said.

When it was dark, the thief returned to town. He went to the shop. The street was almost empty. Only one woman was walking there. The thief smiled to himself.

He did not know the woman was watching him. It was Morgiana. She had seen him smile. She remembered that smile. It belonged to the tricky trader.

The thief marked an **X** on Ali Baba's shop. He dropped the chalk and walked away.

Morgiana guessed the mark meant trouble for Ali Baba. She picked up the chalk. She marked an **X** on all the doors along the street.

The captain and his men arrived later that night. Every door along the street had a chalk mark. The thieves did not know which shop to strike. They were very angry. The captain was the angriest of all.

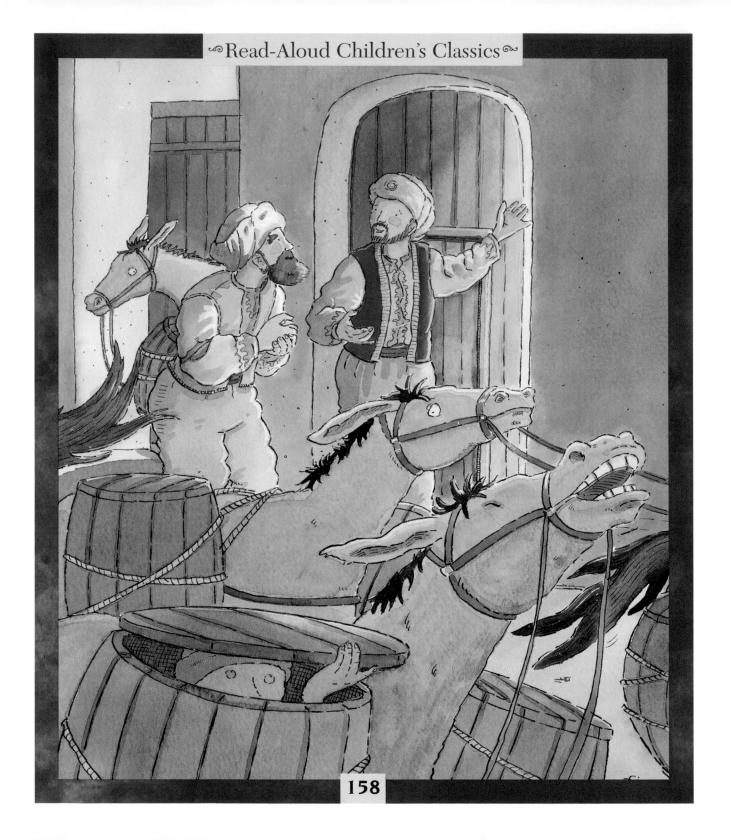

The forty thieves held a meeting the next day.

"Someone figured out our chalk trick," the angry captain said. "I have a plan that will not fail."

He told them his plan.

The thieves lined up twenty mules. Each mule carried two very large oil barrels. All the barrels were empty. The men climbed into them.

The captain screwed the lids on the barrels. He covered his hair with a scarf. He put on a fake beard. He led the mules toward town.

Ali Baba heard a knock on the door of his shop. He opened it to find a man with twenty mules.

"Can I help you?" Ali Baba asked.

"I have come to town to sell my oil," the man said. "There is no room at the inn. I wondered if I might sleep in your stable."

"Your mules can stay in my stable," Ali Baba said. "But I ask that you stay at my house."

The man quickly agreed. Ali Baba took the man home with him.

"Dinner is almost ready," Ali Baba said.

The man took the mules to the stable. He gave each one hay and water. He whispered into each barrel.

"Stay here until you hear my whistle. Then we will attack," he said.

He left the stable and went to the house.

The man was not Ali Baba's only guest. Morgiana was also staying with Ali Baba and his family.

When everyone went to bed, Morgiana could not sleep. She went to the kitchen for some tea. She needed oil to heat the water. There was none left. She thought of the other guest and all his oil. She did not think he would mind if she took some.

She walked to the stable. She turned the lid on one of the barrels. Inside the barrel, a voice whispered.

"Is it time?" the voice asked.

"No, not yet," she whispered back.

Morgiana tested all forty barrels. Whispers came from all but one. Why would men hide in oil barrels? She did not know. She just knew it meant trouble for Ali Baba.

She had to think quickly. She rolled up some hay and set it on fire. She opened the lid of one barrel.

"Go quietly or this fire goes in with you," she said.

The man jumped out and ran. She went to every barrel and said the same thing. She scared all the men away.

The captain came out. He whistled. All was quiet. He checked all of the barrels. He found that they were empty. He knew he had been found out.

He ran, too.

Ali Baba thanked Morgiana for being so brave. He wanted to reward her. He made her a partner at the shop. He also hired guards for protection.

The captain watched Ali Baba and his guards. He could not believe his plan had failed. He was angry. He was so angry he sent all his men away. He would deal with Ali Baba himself.

The captain shaved his head. He took a new name. He became Hassan. He opened a shop next to Ali Baba's shop. Hassan and Ali Baba became good friends. Ali Baba had no idea who Hassan really was.

"Will you come for dinner?" Ali Baba asked.

"Nothing would make me happier," Hassan said.

Morgiana also came to dinner. She noticed Hassan was wearing a very beautiful robe. She also noticed he kept reaching beneath it. She saw a flash of silver. He was hiding a knife!

Morgiana knew this man. He was the lying oil merchant. She had to do something to protect Ali Baba.

"Ali Baba," she said, "I must dance for your friend."

She danced with scarves. She circled the chair where Hassan sat. She tied him up tightly with the scarves.

Morgiana pulled the knife out from Hassan's robe.

"This man wants to hurt you, Ali Baba," she said. "He is none other than the lying oil merchant."

Ali Baba's guards took Hassan to jail. They came back with big news. Hassan was a famous thief. He was the captain of the forty thieves.

Everything became clear to Ali Baba. The captain knew he had robbed the hideout. He wanted to hurt Ali Baba and his family in return. The captain had failed because Morgiana was so smart.

"Morgiana, you saved my family," Ali Baba said.

"You would have done the same for me," she said.

The police chief visited Ali Baba's house. Many towns had been robbed by the forty thieves.

"Each town offered money to anyone who caught them," the chief said. "You have done so. All that money is yours."

He gave Ali Baba a heavy bag. It was filled with coins. Ali Baba knew just what to do with it.

He gave it to Morgiana.

"I want you to have this money," he said.

"I cannot take it," she said. "This money would make your life perfect. You could even open another shop."

"My life is already perfect," he said. "Money cannot buy good friends like you. Take it and open your own shop."

Morgiana did. She opened a shop next to Ali Baba's shop. She worked hard. She was a good friend. She was very happy.

Rikki-Tikki-Tavi

Adapted by Brian Conway ▪ Illustrated by Richard Bernal

This is the story of a brave little mongoose. His name was Rikki-Tikki-Tavi. Every mongoose is little, fast, and furry. But not one is as brave as Rikki-Tikki-Tavi.

Rikki-Tikki-Tavi lived in India. He lived inside a hill in the jungle. A hole inside the hill was his home. One day, a big flood rushed through the jungle. It swept Rikki-Tikki-Tavi out of his hole. The rushing water carried him away.

Rikki-Tikki-Tavi bumped and rolled with the water. He thrashed his long, bushy tail. He was brave, but he could not fight the flood.

The flood was over in a flash. Rikki-Tikki-Tavi had been washed away. He was far from his home. His back hurt. His head hurt. Even the tip of his long tail hurt. He lay there in a puddle for a long time. He was weak. He could barely move.

Rikki-Tikki-Tavi heard voices around him.

"Something died in the road," a boy said.

"Is it a cat, Teddy?" asked his mother.

"I think it's a rat," said Teddy.

Rikki-Tikki-Tavi lifted his head a bit.

"It's a mongoose," said Teddy's father.

"A mongoose?" asked Teddy. "I have never seen one before."

"It is still alive, but just barely," said Teddy's father

The boy picked Rikki-Tikki-Tavi up from the mud. He wrapped him in his shirt and carried him home. His parents brought out a towel for him.

Rikki-Tikki-Tavi was wet and cold. The soft, dry towel warmed him up.

"Rub the towel over his fur, Teddy," said the boy's mother. "The little guy is soaked through."

Rikki-Tikki-Tavi liked being under the towel. He felt safe there. The towel tickled his nose. He let out a sneeze. He shook the last few drops of muddy water from his fur. Teddy and his mother and father laughed.

Rikki-Tikki-Tavi started to feel better. He poked his head out from under the towel. He looked around. His new friends looked very kind.

Rikki-Tikki-Tavi brushed his little pink nose against Teddy's chin.

"Hey, that tickles," Teddy said.

"He wants to be your friend," said Teddy's father.

"Can I keep him?" Teddy asked.

"He is a wild animal," his mother said.

"You can't keep a wild animal," his father said. "He will go wherever he wants to go."

Rikki-Tikki-Tavi ducked back under the towel for a little nap.

"Well, it looks like this is where he wants to be," Teddy's father said.

Everyone laughed again. Rikki-Tikki-Tavi liked that. It made him feel much better.

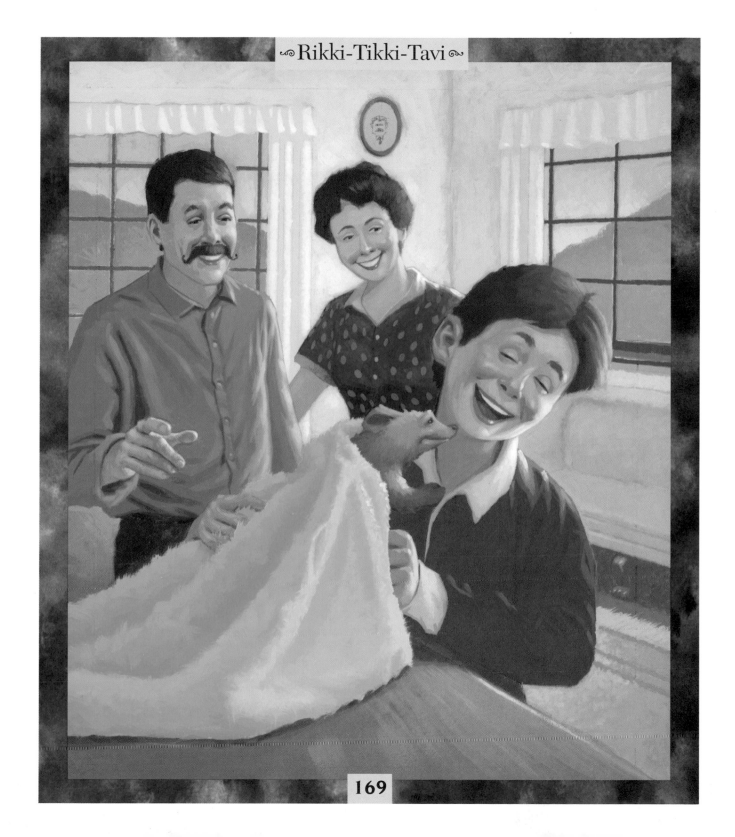

Rikki-Tikki-Tavi liked Teddy's house. It was warm and clean. Teddy was always willing to play with him. At bedtime, he crawled under the covers to sleep beside Teddy.

Rikki-Tikki-Tavi still wanted to do the things a wild mongoose did. He liked to play in the garden. He especially liked to run under the rosebushes and through the grass.

In the garden, Rikki-Tikki-Tavi made many new animal friends. His best friend was Darzee. She was a beautiful songbird.

"Am I the only mongoose around?" he asked Darzee.

"I have never seen anyone quite like you," Darzee said.

Rikki-Tikki-Tavi felt special. He was the only mongoose around. He liked the idea of being the only mongoose around. He ran back through the yard. The garden was his own little jungle kingdom.

Suddenly, Rikki-Tikki-Tavi heard Darzee shriek. He rushed to the tree where she lived.

"My egg!" she cried. "It fell from my nest, and Nag slithered off with it!"

"Who is Nag?" asked Rikki-Tikki-Tavi.

Rikki-Tikki-Tavi heard a low hiss behind him. He turned with a start.

A big, deadly snake looked down on him.

"Who is Nag?" the snake hissed. "I am Nag!"

The snake had angry red eyes. It stared at Rikki-Tikki-Tavi.

"My family has ruled this garden for thousands of years," Nag said. "Every animal here must fear me."

Rikki-Tikki-Tavi was not afraid of Nag. Nag was a cobra. Cobras were one of the deadliest snakes in the world. But Rikki-Tikki-Tavi was a mongoose. A mongoose is not afraid of cobras.

"I do not fear you, Nag," Rikki-Tikki-Tavi said.

Rikki-Tikki-Tavi was ready to fight. His eyes turned a deep red just like Nag's eyes.

Nag had a surprise of his own. There were two big snakes living in the garden. Nag had a wife. Her name was Nagaina. She appeared right behind Rikki-Tikki-Tavi. She also had angry red eyes.

"Look out!" yelled Darzee.

Nagaina struck at Rikki-Tikki-Tavi with her fangs. Rikki-Tikki-Tavi hopped out of her way. The two snakes escaped by sliding away into the tall grass.

That night, Teddy and his parents slept. Rikki-Tikki-Tavi stayed awake. He peeked his head out from under Teddy's warm covers. He heard the sound of snakes moving along the rug. He also heard voices.

Rikki-Tikki-Tavi went towards the bathroom. The snakes were whispering in the dark. Rikki-Tikki-Tavi crept closer until he could hear what they were saying. He listened carefully.

Nag and Nagaina were making evil plans.

"We must scare the big ones away," Nag whispered. "The people will be gone. There will be no one to help the little mongoose."

"Then the garden will be ours again," Nagaina said. "Our eggs will hatch soon. We will raise our children to rule this place."

"We will rule for a thousand more years," Nag said.

Rikki-Tikki-Tavi's eyes glowed a deep red. He did not like the snakes in the house.

"Go into the bedroom," Nagaina told Nag. "I will wait outside. When the people come running out, I will be waiting."

"We will take care of the mongoose together," Nag said.

"It will be a pleasure," Nagaina said.

Nagaina slithered out to the yard. Nag slithered toward the bedrooms.

Rikki-Tikki-Tavi watched Nag move away. He had to be sure to be quiet. He crept up behind him. He used his quick little legs to leap up. He landed on the snake's neck.

Nag twisted and turned. He whipped his head around. Rikki-Tikki-Tavi held on to his neck. He did not want the cobra's fangs to reach him.

Rikki-Tikki-Tavi bit the snake. He would not let go. Nag hissed.

Rikki-Tikki-Tavi held on. The snake could not shake him off.

Rikki-Tikki-Tavi heard a loud sound. He did not know what happened, but Nag's body went limp.

Rikki-Tikki-Tavi saw Teddy's father standing right over them. He had a broomstick. He had hit Nag over the head with it. He dropped it and picked up Rikki-Tikki-Tavi. The brave mongoose was not harmed.

"Teddy!" his mother called. "Your mongoose has just saved our lives!"

Rikki-Tikki-Tavi knew he would have to fight Nagaina. She would find out Nag was dead and want revenge. She would hurt Rikki-Tikki-Tavi's family.

Rikki-Tikki-Tavi made sure his family was safe. Then he went outside. He found Darzee in the garden. He told her how he had beaten Nag. He told her how he planned to send Nagaina away.

"I am going to find Nagaina's eggs," Rikki-Tikki-Tavi said. "You must help me by keeping Nagaina busy."

"I will keep her away for as long as I can," Darzee said.

Darzee hopped towards the house. Nagaina was crying near the porch.

"Oh, my," Darzee said. "My wing is broken. I cannot fly."

Nagaina heard Darzee's cries. She slithered towards the bird. Darzee hopped away from the house. She hopped away from the garden. Nagaina followed her. She did not know Darzee was pretending.

Rikki-Tikki-Tavi waited for Nagaina to leave the garden. Then he carried her eggs away. Darzee flew over him when he had the last egg.

"Hurry, Rikki-Tikki-Tavi!" she said. "Nagaina is on the porch! She has trapped Teddy and his family!"

Rikki-Tikki-Tavi ran as fast as he could to the house.

Nagaina was ready to strike. She turned first towards Teddy.

"I have the last of your eggs here," Rikki-Tikki-Tavi said. "I hid the rest."

Nagaina snapped at Rikki-Tikki-Tavi. He leapt away from her deadly fangs. He was quick. Her tail hit the egg. The egg rolled off the porch.

Before Rikki-Tikki-Tavi could stop her, Nagaina slid towards her egg. She snatched it up in her mouth and slithered away.

Rikki-Tikki-Tavi ran as fast as he could. He was close behind Nagaina.

Nagaina slid into her hole. Rikki-Tikki-Tavi grabbed her tail and held on. Nagaina dragged him down into the hole. She dropped her egg. He grabbed her head. If she moved, she would crush her last egg.

"I will not harm you or your family," Rikki-Tikki-Tavi said. "But you must promise you will not harm my family."

"Where are my eggs?" Nagaina hissed.

"I put them in the meadow beside the river," Rikki-Tikki-Tavi answered. "They are safe. Get them and never come back here."

Nagaina took her egg and left. She would not come back.

Teddy and his parents had saved Rikki-Tikki-Tavi after the flood. He had returned their kindness. He lived with them for a long time. He spent the nights under Teddy's warm covers. He spent his days playing in the garden. It was his own little jungle kingdom.

❧ The Golden Goose ❧

Adapted by Jennifer Boudart ▪ Illustrated by Karen Dugan

A little log cabin stood in the middle of a forest. It was home to a young boy named Samuel. He lived with his mother, father, and two older brothers.

Samuel was a kind and gentle boy. He tried very hard not to make trouble. He stayed out of the way of the others. He did what he was told. He tried to do everything well. He tried as hard as he could. But his family always found fault with him.

"You forgot to sweep under the beds," his mother always said.

"You water the plants too much," his father always said.

"You chew like a cow," his brother Tom always said.

"You hog all the covers," his brother Jack always said.

Samuel never said anything back. He just put his head down. He kept his mouth shut. He did not like to make things worse.

One day, he sat shelling nuts. They always left him alone when he was shelling nuts.

"Who will go chop some wood?" his mother asked.

Samuel did not offer to go. He knew his mother would just laugh.

"I will go," Tom said.

"Good boy," said their mother.

She kissed Tom's cheek and gave him a basket. It was filled with sweet cakes and cold lemonade. Tom took an axe and headed into the woods.

It was not long before Tom returned home. He had the axe and the lunch basket. He did not have any wood. One of his shoulders was bleeding.

"What happened, Tom?" their mother asked.

"It wasn't my fault!" Tom said. "I met a strange man in the woods. He was old and wrinkled. He started the trouble. He asked for food. Can you believe that? He wanted to get his dirty hands on my lunch!"

"What did you tell him?" Samuel asked.

He hoped Tom had helped the man.

"I told him no, of course!" Tom said. "I said there were only enough sweet cakes for me."

Tom explained what had happened next.

"I ordered the old man to get out of my way. I began chopping wood. I lost my hold on the axe. It cut my shoulder."

"What did the old man do?" Samuel asked.

"Nothing," Tom said. "He just looked happy."

Samuel could understand that. Tom had been rude to the old man. His shoulder had only a scratch. It was not even bleeding anymore.

"I will go and chop the wood," Jack said.

"Good boy," said their mother.

She kissed Jack's cheek and gave him the basket. Plenty of sweet cakes and lemonade were left. Jack took the axe and went on his way.

It was not long before Jack returned home. He carried the lunch basket. He did not have the axe. He did not have the wood. His foot was bleeding.

"What happened, Jack?" their mother asked.

"It wasn't my fault!" Jack said. "I went to finish Tom's work. That strange old man was there. Tom was right. He is a troublemaker. He asked for a drink. He wanted to get his wormy lips on my clean jug!"

"What did you tell him?" Samuel asked.

He could guess the answer.

"I told him no, of course!" Jack said. "I told him there was only enough lemonade for me."

"Did you get hurt chopping wood, too?" asked Samuel.

"Yes I did, you fool," Jack said. "Somehow, the axe broke in two pieces. The blade cut my foot. That man just sat there and looked happy."

Samuel could understand that.

"I will go chop the wood," Samuel said.

His family stared at him. They laughed at him.

"Be careful not to get chopped in half," his father said.

"Silly boy," his mother said.

She did not kiss him. She did not give him sweet cakes and lemonade. He wrapped some bread and a water jug in a cloth. He picked up a new axe and went on his way.

Samuel whistled as he walked. He was not afraid to meet the old man. He wanted to meet him. He wanted to say he was sorry for his brothers. They had not been very nice.

Samuel saw Jack's broken axe on the ground. The old man sat nearby.

"Hello," he said. "I am Samuel. I think you have already met my brothers. I am sorry they were rude."

"It is not your fault," the old man said. "Will you sit with me?"

Samuel nodded and sat down.

He could see the man was very old and wrinkled. His skin made Samuel think of walnut shells. He seemed nice. His hands were not dirty. His lips were not wormy either.

"I am very thirsty and hungry," the man said. "Will you share your lunch with me?"

"Oh, yes," Samuel said. "I wish I had something good to share. I have only dry bread and warm water."

Samuel untied his cloth. It was filled with sweet cakes and a full jug of lemonade. He could not believe it! He knew he had packed bread and water.

"What luck!" he said. "We will eat well!"

Samuel and the old man ate all the sweet cakes. They drank all the lemonade. It was a good lunch.

The old man had many stories to share. He was really very nice.

"It is time for me to go," the old man said.

Samuel did not want to say good-bye. He was having such a nice time. But he showed the man the direction of the town. He said he was sorry again for his brothers.

"I have been thinking about that," said the old man. "You are not at all like your brothers. You shared your lunch with me. You kept me company when you could have been chopping wood. You are a very kind young man."

Samuel looked down at his feet. He did not know what to say. He was not used to hearing nice words.

"I would like to repay your kindness," said the old man. "Do you see the tree with the axe marks in it?"

Samuel nodded. He saw where Tom and Jack had chopped at it.

"I kept your brothers from chopping the tree down," said the old man. "I think you should finish what they started. Look inside the tree once you cut it in two. You will find something."

The man started down the road. Samuel began to chop at the tree. His strokes were strong and sure. The tree fell with a crash. Samuel looked down into the stump.

A goose was curled up inside.

Samuel gently lifted it out. He held it in his arms. It was smooth and soft. Its feathers were golden!

The goose was special. Samuel could not take it home. He needed to find the old man for help. Samuel ran to the road. There was no sign of the old man. He started towards town.

The people on the road thought the golden goose was quite a sight.

Three sisters saw the goose. They had to touch it to see if it was real. They touched the goose at the same time. They could not pull away. All the sisters were stuck to the goose and to each other!

"Stop trying to steal that goose," a judge said to the girls. He grabbed the last girl in line. He got stuck, too.

"Leave my girls alone," the mother of the girls said.

She grabbed the judge's coat. She also got stuck.

Samuel noticed none of this. The line of people behind him grew. When he got to the town he saw the people acting strange. Some were making funny faces. Some were throwing pies at each other.

"The princess cannot laugh," a man said to Samuel. "The king promises half his land to whoever makes her laugh."

Samuel saw the king and the princess on the balcony. He decided to ask the princess why she was unhappy. He knew what it was like to be unhappy.

The princess looked down. What she saw looked like a giant, wiggly worm. It was made of many people and one golden goose. The princess watched them tug and pull and twist. She started to laugh!

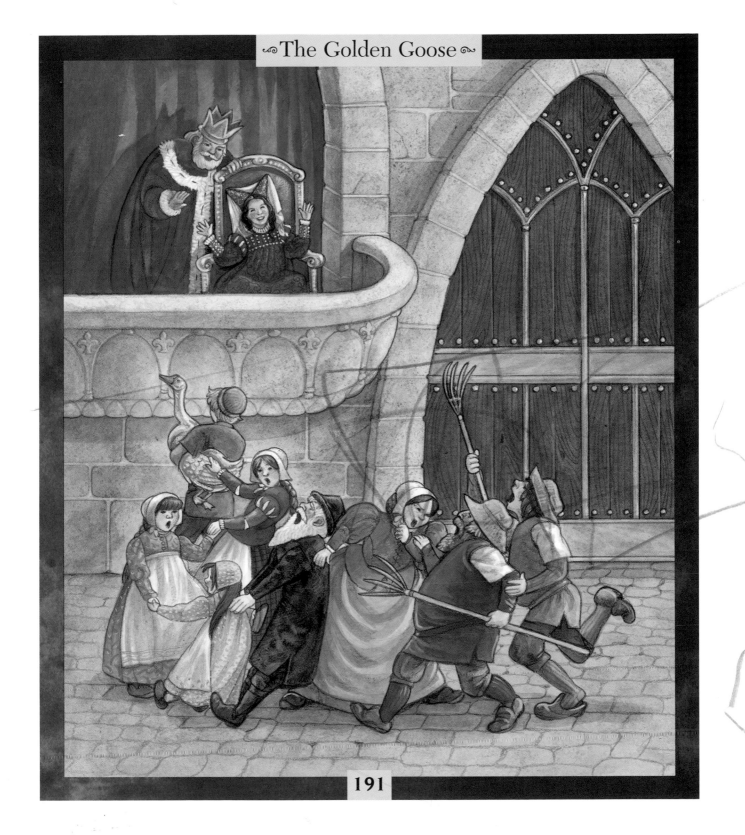

The princess laughed and laughed. She fell off of her chair.

"Who made my wish come true?" the king asked.

Samuel saw the princess point to him. He was sure she was pointing at someone else. He turned around to look. He saw everyone behind him for the first time. It made him laugh, too.

"How did you do this?" the princess asked Samuel.

"I do not know," Samuel said. "I found this special goose in the forest. A friend helped me. I am trying to find that friend."

"You say this is a special goose?" asked the king. "What makes it special? What causes such sticky problems?"

"It was a test," said a voice in the crowd.

It was the old man.

"The goose is under a magic spell," he said. "The hand that touches it in disbelief will stick to its feathers. Samuel believed such a goose could exist. He also believed in me. He did not stick to the goose. Everyone else did."

The old man touched each person stuck to the golden goose. Each one finally came free. He lifted the goose from Samuel's arms.

"Go claim the king's reward," the old man said. "I must go."

Samuel would miss him. They were friends.

"You must come and visit," Samuel said. "I will have half of the king's land. There will be plenty to share."

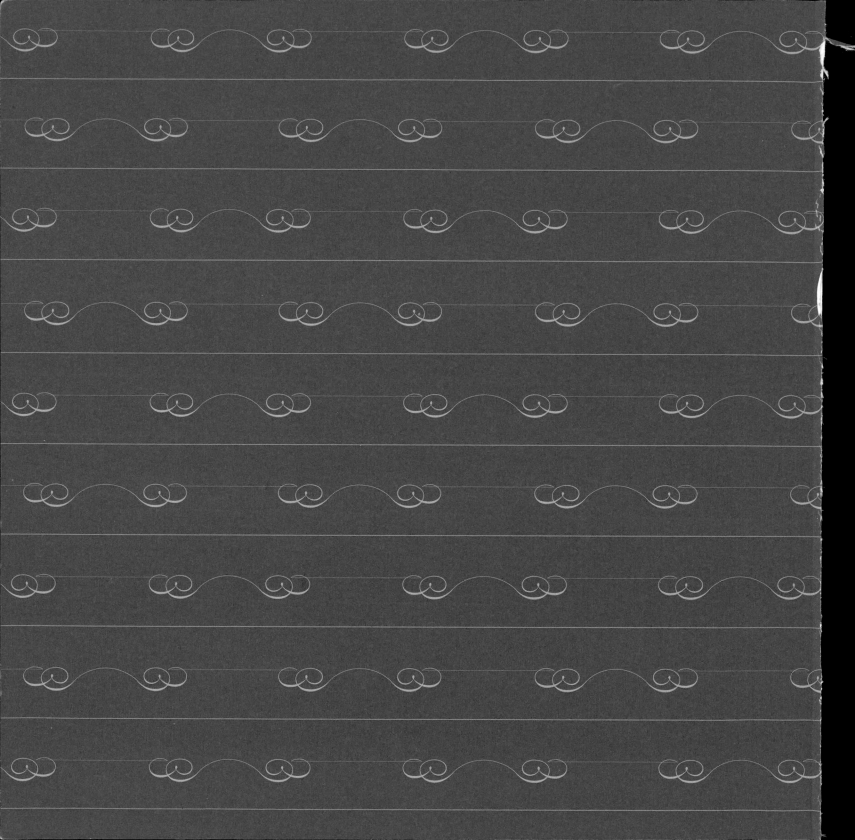